The Monk's Wedding

ii

The Monk's Wedding

by Conrad Ferdinand Meyer

A new American translation by David Staats

Table of Contents

Translator's Preface

Swiss author Conrad Ferdinand Meyer (1825 – 1898) was a master of the historical novella. *The Monk's Wedding*, written in 1884, besides being good story-telling, shows an intriguing and skillful use of the frame narration technique. The frame narrative, which tells the story of Dante telling the story of the monk's wedding, takes place at the court of an Italian nobleman of Verona, Cangrande della Scala (1291 – 1329). Cangrande was a historical personage who was a patron of the poet Dante Alighieri (1265 – 1321). The frame narrative takes place probably sometime between the years 1312 and 1318, when Dante would have been about 50.

In the story of the monk's wedding which Dante tells, another historical personage, Ezzelino III da Romano (1194 – 1259), figures prominently. Ezzelino ruled Padua in the early to mid 1200's with what has been considered proverbial cruelty and arbitrariness. Based on Ezzelino's involvement, we can say that the story of the monk's wedding probably takes place about the year 1230.

Both Cangrande and Ezzelino are mentioned by Dante in his *Divine Comedy*. He speaks favorably of Cangrande in *Paradiso*, Canto XVII, lines 70-93. Ezzelino, on the other hand, is consigned to hell. We meet him in *Inferno*, Canto XII, line 109.

* * *

My aim in this translation, however imperfectly realized, was to make a translation from which an English speaker would receive the same impression as a German speaker would receive from reading the original. Naturally this involved the comprehension of the thought as expressed in the original German, and the rendering of that thought into English, rather than a mere substitution of English words for German words. But it also involved more. For example, it requires a refusal to make the translation more clear than the original. If a German reader would have to pause and reflect for a moment upon reading a sentence in order to get the author's meaning, then it would be an error in translation to make the meaning of the English rendering instantly obvious to an English reader. The ideal, patently unattainable, would be to make the nature and duration of the pause similar for readers of congruent education and fluency in each language.

A similar challenge, arising not infrequently in this translation, occurs when words between languages may match in meaning but not in level of diction, or vice-versa. Suppose, for example, that a word in the German is of an elevated diction, typically used only in formal settings, and that it might possibly be translated by either of two English words, one of which matches the meaning precisely, but is colloquial or slang, and the other matches the level of diction precisely, but has slightly different connotations. Which to use? The problem is made more complex when one takes into account that the meaning and level of diction, and indeed other characteristics of a word, are influenced by the words which surround the word under examination. In this translation, I have tried to accurately render both meaning and diction, but where there was an irreconcilable conflict, I have given preference to more accurately rendering the meaning at the expense of matching tone or diction.

The Monk's Wedding

It was in Verona. In front of a large fire that filled a spacious fireplace, young servants, male and female, were arranged in the most comfortable positions consistent with decorum, around an equally young prince and two blossoming young women. This princely group sat to the left of the fireplace, and the others surrounded them in a quarter circle, leaving the entire other side of the fireplace unoccupied, according to the custom of the court. The lord was that poet whom they call Cangrande. Of the women in the middle of whom he sat, the one nearest the fireplace, leaning back somewhat and half in the dark, may have been his wife, and the other, fully illuminated, a relative or friend; and stories were being told accompanied by knowing glances and soft laughter.

Now into this sensual and licentious group came a grave man, whose large features and long robes appeared to be out of another world. "Sir, I have come to warm myself at your fireplace," said the strange man, half formally, half scornfully, and he did not disdain to add that the careless servants, in spite of the frosty November evening had forgotten or neglected to light a fire in the guest's upper room.

"Sit next to me, my Dante," replied Cangrande, "but if you want sociably to warm yourself, then don't stare silently into the fire as is your wont. We are telling stories here, and the hand which was today devising terza rima[1]   – as I was going up to my astrology chamber I heard from your room verses being scanned in a dull singsong – this imposing hand dare not today refuse to take in its fingers the trivial task of devising a short narrative without any interruption. Take a break from the goddesses" – of course he meant the muses – "and enjoy yourself with these lovely mortals." The descendant of the house of Scaligeri indicated to his guest with a faint movement of his hand the two women, of whom the taller, who apparently was sitting insensately in the shadow, did not think it necessary to move over, while the smaller and alert young woman promptly made room for the Florentine next to her. However, he did not comply with the invitation of his host, but haughtily chose the last seat, at the end of the little circle. Either he did not care for the bigamy of his host – even if it was only the amusement of an evening – or he was disgusted by the court jester, who with his legs stretched out, sat next to Cangrande's chair on the latter's coat which had slipped to the floor.

This jester, an old, toothless man with bug-eyes and a drooping, gossipy, greedy mouth – next to Dante the

---

1

A form of verse with three lines per stanza – in which Dante wrote the *Divine Comedy*. [Translator's footnote]

only elderly person in the group – was called Gocciola, that is, droplet, because he used to collect and slurp down the last sticky drops from the empty glasses, and hated the stranger with a childish malice because he saw in Dante a rival for the none-too-particular favor of the lord. He made a face, and grinning derisively was happy to point out to the pretty neighbor at his left the poet's shadowed profile against the light ceiling of the high-ceilinged room. Dante's silhouette resembled a giant hag with a long bent nose and sagging lips – a Fate or something similar. The lively maid gave a childish laugh. Her neighbor, a sharp-looking lad named Ascanio, caused her to stifle her laugh, in that he spoke to Dante with that moderate deference with which the latter loved to be addressed.

"Do not disdain it, you who are the Homer and Virgil of Italy," he said, "to join in our harmless little game. Condescend to us and tell a story instead of singing."

"What is your theme?" threw out Dante, less unsociably than at first, but still sullenly enough.

"Sudden change in profession," replied the youth succinctly, "with a good or a bad or a ridiculous outcome."

Dante thought for a moment. His melancholy eyes were regarding the company, whose composition did not seem to entirely displease him; for he discovered therein, next to several low foreheads a few imposing

ones. "Has any of you treated of the defrocked monk?"
said the somewhat mollified poet.

"Certainly, Dante," replied a knight with an open
face named Germano, pronouncing his Italian with a
slight German accent, and who was wearing chain mail
and a long drooping mustache. "I myself told the story
of the young Manuccio, who jumped over the walls of
his monastery to become a warrior."

"He did the right thing," said Dante, "he had
deceived himself about his disposition."

"I, master," prattled in her turn a saucy, rather
voluptuous woman of Padua, Isotta by name, "told the
story of Helena Manente, who lightly threw away the
first lock of hair taken off by the consecrated scissors,
but quickly covered the rest with both hands and
swallowed her nun's vows, for she had espied in the
nave of the church her boyfriend, who had fallen into
and was miraculously rescued from the most barbaric
slavery, as he was hanging his broken chains" – she was
going to say, on the wall, but her nonsense was cut short
by the mouth of Dante.

"She did well," he said, "for she acted out of the
reality of her enamored nature. I am not talking about
such stuff, but rather of a quite different case: namely if
a monk, not of his own initiative, not out of awakened
worldly desire, not because he mistook his nature, but
rather for the sake of another, under the pressure of an
alien will, even if perhaps out of sanctified grounds of

piety, is false to himself, breaks himself even more than the vows he gave the church, and throws off the habit which fitted him well and did not burden him. Did someone tell that story? No? Then I will tell it. But tell me, what will be the end of such a matter, my patron and protector?" He had turned to face Cangrande directly.

"Necessarily bad," immediately answered the other. "Whoever leaps of his free will, leaps well; whoever is pushed, leaps badly."

"You speak the truth, master," confirmed Dante, "and nothing different intended the Apostle, if I understand him, when he writes: that sin is whatever does not proceed from faith, that is from the conviction and truth of our nature."

"Do there even have to be monks?" snickered a muffled voice from the shadows, as if it wanted to say: every release from an inherently unnatural state is a good deed.

The brash and heretical remark aroused no indignation here, for at this court the boldest speeches about ecclesiastical matters were tolerated, even greeted with smiles, whereas a free or even careless word about the ruler, his person or his politics, could be ruinous.

Dante's eye sought the speaker and discovered him in a distinguished young cleric, whose fingers played with the precious cross which he wore over his priestly garments.

"Not as far as I am concerned," answered the Florentine slowly. "The monks can die out just as soon as a race is resurrected which can unite the two greatest powers of humanity, which seem to be incompatible, justice and mercy. Until that far off time, let the state take care of the one, and the church the other. Since, however, the exercise of mercy requires a thoroughly selfless soul, the three monastic vows[2] are justified; because it is less difficult, as experience teaches, to renounce desire entirely, rather than halfway."

"But aren't there more bad monks than good ones?" returned the clerical doubter.

"No," asserted Dante, "when you take human weakness into account. Otherwise, there would be more unjust judges than just ones, more cowardly warriors than brave ones, more bad people than good."

"And isn't that the case?" whispered the man in the shadows.

"No," said Dante decisively, and a heavenly transfiguration illumined his stern features. "Doesn't our philosophy investigate and seek to answer how evil came into the world? If evil ones were in the majority, we would ask: how came good into the world?"

2

Poverty, chastity, obedience. [Translator's footnote]

These haughty and deep phrases impressed the company, but also aroused the concern that the Florentine might burrow into his scholastic inquiries rather than into his story.

Cangrande saw the way his young lady friend employed a dainty yawn. Under these circumstances, he seized the floor and asked, "Are you going to tell us a true story, my Dante, one that's documented, or a legend from the oral tradition, or an invention from your own bewreathed head?

The latter answered with slow emphasis, "I shall develop my story from an epitaph."

"From an epitaph?"

"From an epitaph which I read years ago at the Franciscans in Padua. The gravestone on which it was written lay in a corner of the cloister, indeed hidden under a wild rosebush, but still accessible to the novices if they were willing to crawl on all fours and not be afraid of a few scratches on their faces. I ordered the prior – I mean, I requested him, to remove the stone in question to the library and place it under the watch of an old man."

"Well, what did the stone say?" The prince's wife languidly allowed herself a question.

"The inscription," replied Dante, "was in Latin and read: *Hic jacet monachus Astorre cum uxore Antiope. Sepeliebat Azzolinus.*"

"What does that mean?" asked the other woman eagerly.

Cangrande translated fluently, "Here lies the monk Astorre with his wife Antiope. Ezzelino buried them both."

"The odious tyrant!' exclaimed the sensitive woman. "Of course he had them both buried alive because they loved each other, and ridiculed their sacrifice even in the grave by calling her the monk's wife. The cruel brute!"

"Hardly," said Dante. "To my mind it happened otherwise, and it is also unlikely according to history. For Ezzelino was more a threat to ecclesiastical discipline than he was a punisher of the breaking of sacred vows. I take the word "*sepeliebat*" in a friendly sense: he gave the two of them a burial."

"Right," cried Cangrande happily. "You think as I do, Florentine! Ezzelino was a ruler by nature, and as such persons are, somewhat rough and violent. Nine tenths of his crimes were invented by priests and superstitious peasants."

"Would that it were so!" sighed Dante. "Where he elsewhere appears in my tale he is not yet the monster which history, rightly or wrongly, depicts him; rather, his brutality only first begins to show itself, as a line around the mouth, so to speak –"

"A commanding figure." Cangrande completed the picture excitedly. "with bristling black forelock, like you depicted him in your twelfth canto as a denizen of hell. Where did you get this black-haired head?"

"That's your head," replied Dante daringly, and Cangrande felt flattered.

"And the other figures of the story," he continued with a menacing smile, "I will – you will permit me?" and he turned to the surrounding listeners – "take from among you and give them your names: your interior lives I won't touch, because I cannot read them."

"My countenance I freely give you ," grandly said the princess, whose indifference had begun to soften.

A buzz of the greatest excitement ran through the listeners, and: "Your story, Dante!" was murmured from all sides. "Your story!"

"Here it is," he said, and told his story.

Where the course of the Brenta approaches the city of Padua in a narrow bend, without actually touching the city, on one glorious summer day a festooned boat accompanied by muted flute music and overloaded with festively dressed people glided on the rapid but quiet water. Umberto Vicedomini was bringing home his bride, Diana Pizzaguerra. The Paduan had fetched his fiancée from a cloister on the upper reaches of the river, where, by an old custom of the city, young women of rank were wont to withdraw before their marriage for the purpose of exercises in piety. She sat in the middle of the boat on a purple cushion between her bridegroom and the three thriving boys from his first marriage. Umberto Vicedomino had buried the wife of his youth five years ago, when the plague raged in Padua, and even though he was in the prime of manhood had decided upon this second marriage only with difficulty and grudgingly, upon the daily cajoling of an old and ailing father.

The boat ran on with shipped oars, giving itself over to the way of the stream. The oarsmen accompanied the soft music with a low chant. Then both became silent. All eyes were directed to the right bank, on which a tall rider was restraining his stallion and with a broad gesture waving to the boat. An awestruck murmur ran through the rows of passengers. The rowers tore their red caps from their heads, and the entire company rose in fear and deference, even the groom, Diana, and the boys. Subservient gestures, waving arms, half-bent knees addressed themselves to the shore with such vehemence and excess of movement that the boat lost its balance, tilted to the right and suddenly capsized. A cry of horror, a swirling vortex, and a vacant stream populated by surfacing and re-submerging persons and the floating wreathes of the ill-fated boat. Help was not far, since a little further downstream was a small port where fishermen and bargemen stayed and even today were waiting for the steeds and sedan chairs which the company, that now was sinking in the stream, ultimately were to have brought to Padua.

The first two rescue boats rushed toward each other from opposite shores. In the one, Ezzelino, the tyrant of Padua, the innocent cause of the catastrophe, stood next to an old ferryman with a shaggy beard; in the other, approaching from the left bank, a young monk and his ferryman, who thrust his small, dusty wooden boat out into the stream just at that moment when the calamity occurred. The two boats reached one another. Between them a mass of blond hair floated in the river; the monk grabbed it, kneeling with outstretched arm, while his boatman leaned out of the other side of the boat for all he was worth. At the end of a thick skein the monk raised up a head, which kept its eyes closed, and then, with the help of the near approaching Ezzelino, lifted out of the current the burden of a woman weighed down with sopping clothes. The tyrant had leaped from his dinghy into the other and now regarded the lifeless head, which bore an expression of defiance and sorrow, with a certain satisfaction, whether at the magnificent features of that head, or at the quietude of death.

"Do you know her, Astorre?" he asked the monk. The latter shook his head, and the former continued, "Look, it is the wife of your brother."

The monk gave a pitying, timid glance at the pallid face, which, as he watched, slowly opened its sleeping eyes.

"Take her to the shore!" commanded Ezzelino, as the monk left her alone with his boatman. "I am going to look for my brother," he called, "until I find him." "I'll help you, monk," said the tyrant, "although I doubt that we'll save him: I saw him as he grabbed his boys and, with the three clutching him, sank deep into the water."

In the meantime, the Brenta had become covered with boats. Men fished with poles, gaffs, fishing rods and nets, and in the rapidly changing scene the form of the sovereign was seen everywhere over the searchers and the things they raised up.

"Come, monk!" he said finally. "There is nothing more you can do here. Umberto and his boys have been too long in the water to reappear alive. The stream carried them off. It will deposit them on the bank when it is tired of them. Do you see those tents there?" A number of them had been set up on the bank of the Brenta to receive those expected to accompany the wedding boat, and in which the dead or apparently dead now were being placed, who already were being mourned by the relatives and servants who had rushed out from nearby Padua. "There, monk, do what belongs to your office: works of mercy! comfort the living! bury the dead!"

The monk had stepped onto the shore and had lost sight of the imperial governor. Out of the crowd Diana approached him, the bride and widow of his brother, disconsolate, but having regained control of herself.

Her thick hair was still dripping, but onto a different dress: a compassionate woman from among the common people had given her own dress to her in the tent and had taken possession of the costly wedding dress. "Devout brother," said she to Astorre, "I am abandoned; in all the confusion, the litter which was intended for me has returned to the town with someone else, living or dead. Take me to the house of my father-in-law, who is your father!"

The young widow was mistaken. Not because of the tumult and confusion, but from cowardice and superstition, had the retainers of the old Vicedomini left her in the lurch. They were afraid to bring to the hot-tempered old man a widow and news of the extinction of his posterity.

Since the monk saw many of his fellow monks busy with compassionate works in the tents and round about, he assented to her request. "Let us go," he said, and fell in with the young woman on the road to the town, the towers and domes of which rose against the blue sky. The road was covered with hundreds who were hurrying to the riverside or returning from the riverside. The two strode, often separated from one another, but always finding each other again, in the middle of the street without speaking, and were already walking through the outskirts of the town where the artisans live. Everywhere – the calamity on the Brenta had aroused the entire population – stood loud chattering or whispering groups which regarded the two, now fortuitously brought together, having lost a brother and a groom, with sympathetic curiosity.

The monk and Diana were figures which every child in Padua knew. Astorre, even if he was not considered a saint, nevertheless had the reputation of an exemplary monk. He could be called the official monk of Padua, the one the people honored and the one they were proud of. And with reason: he had bravely, even joyfully, renounced the privileges of his high nobility and the immense wealth of his family, and devoted his life, without trying to get something in return, to the least and the poorest during times of pestilence or other public dangers. And he was, with his chestnut brown curly hair, soft eyes, and aristocratic bearing, an attractive man, as the people like their saints.

Diana was in her own way not less well-known, not least because of her statuesque figure which the people admired more than her delicate features. Her mother was a German, even a Hohenstauffen, as some maintained, though only by blood, and not by law. Germany and Italy, had as good sisters, together built this grand figure.

However austerely and correctly Diana dealt with her equals, with her inferiors she was condescending, let them tell her their quarrels, gave a crisp and clear answer, and kissed the most raggedy children. She donated and contributed without a second thought, probably because her father, the old Pizzaguerra, was, after the Vicedomini, the richest man in Padua, as well as the most sordid skinflint, and Diana was ashamed of the paternal vice.

So the populace, well-disposed toward Diana, married her every month in their pubs and parlors to some distinguished Paduan, but the reality did not conform to these devout wishes. Three obstacles hindered her becoming a bride: Diana's high and often somber brow; her father's tightfistedness; and the blind allegiance of her brother Germano to the tyrant, whose possible fall must also ruin his loyal servant, bringing the latter's family down after him.

Finally, Umberto Vicedomini, who now lay at the bottom of the Brenta, became engaged to her, without love, as was well known in the town.

Withal, the pair was so lost in their legitimate anguish that they either did not hear or did not care about the busy chattering which followed at their heels. It did not give offense that the monk and the woman were walking together. It appeared proper, since the monk had to comfort her and they indeed had to walk the same way: to the old Vicedomini, as the nearest and most natural messengers of what had happened.

The women bemoaned Diana that she had to marry a man who took her only as a substitute for a dear departed wife, and in the same breath lamented that she had lost this same man before the marriage had even begun.

The men, on the other hand, debated with grave gestures and the most shrewd countenances a burning question which had arisen concerning the four heirs, now drowned in the Brenta, of the leading family in Padua. The fortune of the Vicedomini was proverbial. The head of the family, a man as energetic as he was crafty, who had managed to stay on good terms with both the tyrant of Padua, who had been excommunicated five times, and the church which damned him, had his whole life long not bestirred himself a whit about any public matters, but rather had applied his tough character and magnificent strength of will to a single object: the prosperity and flourishing of his progeny. Now this was destroyed. His eldest son and the grandchildren lay in the Brenta. His second and third sons had disappeared from the earth in this same year of misfortune, the one two months ago, and the other three months ago. The tyrant had used up the elder and left him on one of his remote battlefields. The other, whom the impartial father had made a grand merchant after the Venetian manner, had died on a Levantine coast, bleeding to death on a cross to which pirates had nailed him for the sake of a ransom which came too late. As the fourth son, Astorre, the monk, was left. That the father would spend his dying breath trying to wrest the latter from his monastic vows was something the quick-reckoning Paduans did not doubt for a moment. Whether he would succeed, and whether the monk would consent, was what the excited street was now arguing about.

And they argued ultimately so vociferously and vehemently that even the grieving monk could no longer remain in doubt about whom was meant by the "*egli*" and the "*ella*" which sounded from the congregated groups. Accordingly, more for the sake of his companion than for his own sake, he struck into a shaded grassy lane which was well known to his sandals, since it led along the weathered exterior walls of his monastery. Here it was cool enough to cause shivering, but the horrific news which was pervading Padua had even reached these shadows. From the open windows of the refectory which was built into the thick walls, the dinner conversation of the brothers at the delayed midday meal – the catastrophe on the Brenta had disturbed all times and hours in the town – sounded so fractious and clamorous, so full of "-inibus" and "-atibus" – it was carried on in Latin, or they argued using citations from the decretals – that the monk surmised with little difficulty that here too the same or a similar perplexity was being discussed as in the street. And if he did not acknowledge to himself what they were talking about, still he knew whom they were talking about. But what he did not discover were –

In the midst of speaking, Dante sought out among the listeners the genteel cleric who was hiding behind his neighbor.

– were two burning sunken eyes, which were staring through an opening in the wall at him and the woman at his side. These eyes belonged to an unhappy creature, a derelict monk by the name of Serapion, who, body and soul, chafed in the monastery. With his over-hasty imagination he understood on the spot that his fellow monk Astorre was at the end of his abstaining and fasting according to the rule of Saint Francis, and was furiously envious of the worldly possessions and happiness which the caprice of death had tossed in his lap. He was lurking after the two on their way home, in order to scrutinize their faces and to read therein what Astorre had decided about his status. His glances devoured the woman and clung to her gait.

Astorre directed his steps and those of his sister-in-law to a small plaza ringed by four city palaces and entered with her into the stateliest of them. On a stone bench in the courtyard he saw two resting men, a young German armored from tip to toe, and an aged Saracen. The stretched out German rested his sleeping head of curly blond hair in the lap of the sitting unbeliever, who, likewise sleeping, nodded paternally over him with his snow-white beard. The two belonged to the body guard of Ezzelino, which in imitation of that of his father-in-law, the Emperor Frederick, was composed of Germans and Saracens in equal parts. The tyrant was in the palace. He probably considered it his duty to visit the old Vicedomini. In fact, Astorre and Diana heard on their way up the winding stairs the conversation which Ezzelino in short, calm words carried on with the old man, who, on the other hand, seemed to be quite beside himself, screaming and shouting. Monk and woman remained standing at the entrance to the large room among the pallid retainers. The servants quaked in every limb. The old man had heaped fierce curses on them and then chased them away with clenched fists, because they had delayed bringing him the news from the riverbank and had hardly dared stammer it forth. Moreover, the dreaded approach of the tyrant had petrified these retainers. It was forbidden on penalty of death to announce his coming. Unhindered as a ghost did he enter houses and rooms.

"And you report this so calmly, ogre," raged the old man in his despair, "as if you were telling of the loss of a horse or of a crop. You killed the four, nobody but you! What need had you to go riding at the riverbank just at that time? Why did you have to wave to them across the Brenta? You did it to harm me! Do you hear me?"

"Fate," replied Ezzelino.

"Fate?" screamed the Vicedomini. "Fate and astrology and incantations and cabals and beheadings, women throwing themselves from the battlements to the pavement and a hundred young men shot through with arrows falling off their horses in your loathesome reckless battles, that is your era and governing, Ezzelino, curse you and damn you! And you draw everyone after you in your bloody tracks, all living and dying becomes next to you violent and unnatural, and no one dies in their bed any more as a penitent Christian!"

"You do me an injustice," returned the other. "True, I have nothing to do with the Church. It leaves me indifferent. But I have never hindered you and people like you from associating with it. You know that, else you would not dare to exchange correspondence with the Holy See. What are you turning over in your hand there and hiding the papal seal from me? An indulgence? A Papal letter? Give it to me! Right, a Papal letter! May I read it? You permit me? Your patron, the Holy Father, writes you that should your posterity perish down to your fourth and last son, the monk, then he would be *ipso facto* free of his vows, if he of his own will and free decision returns to the world. Sly fox, how many ounces of gold did this parchment cost you?"

"Will you taunt me?" howled the old man. "What else could I do after the death of my second and third sons? For whom would I have hoarded and saved? For the worms? For you? Do you want to rob me? . . . No?

So help me godfather" – Ezzelino, before he was excommunicated had taken the third boy of the Vicedomini, the same one who had sacrificed himself for him on the battlefield, out of the baptismal font – "help me prevail upon the monk to become worldly again, and take a wife, order him to do it, you almighty one, give him to me in place of the son you slaughtered, cross your fingers for me, if you love me."

"That's none of my concern," returned the tyrant without the least agitation. "Let him do it himself. 'Of his own will' is what the papal letter says. Why should he change his status if he is a good monk, as I believe he is? So that the bloodline of the Vicedomini should not die out? Is that a necessity for the life of the world? Are the Vicedominis indispensable?"

The other now shrieked in raving anger: "You fiend, you murderer of my children! I see through you! You want to bury me and use my money to conduct your insane campaigns!" Then he became aware of his daughter-in-law, who had stepped forward through the attendants across the threshold ahead of the hesitating monk. Despite his bodily weakness he bolted towards her with unsteady steps, grabbed her hands, as if he wanted to hold her responsible for the tragedy which had occurred to them both. "Where are you keeping my son, Diana?" he gasped.

"He is lying in the Brenta," she replied, sadly, and her blue eyes darkened.

"Where are my three grandsons?"

"In the Brenta," she repeated.

"And you bring me yourself as a present. You I get to keep?" The old man laughed discordantly.

"Would to God," she said slowly, "the waves had drawn me under and the others stood here instead of me!"

She was silent. Then she fell into a sudden fury. "If the sight of me offends you and if I am a vexation to you, know this: he grabbed me by the hair, when I was already dead, and pulled me back into life."

Now the old man saw for the first time his son, the monk, and his mental faculties pulled themselves together with a strength and rapidity which the bitter sorrow seemed more to have steeled than weakened.

"Really? He retrieved you from the Brenta? Hmm. Remarkable! The ways of God are mysterious indeed!"

He grabbed the monk by the arm and shoulder, as if he wanted to take possession of him body and soul, and dragged him and himself over to his invalid's chair, into which he fell without letting go of the tightly squeezed arm of his unresisting son. Diana followed and knelt by the other side of the chair with drooping arms and folded hands, laying her head on the arm of the chair so that only the top knot of her blond hair remained visible, like an inanimate object. Across from this group sat Ezzelino, resting his right hand on the rolled up papal brief like a field marshall's mace.

"My son, my son," whimpered the old man with a tenderness made up of a mixture of sincerity and craftiness, "my last and only comfort! You stay and support of my old age, you won't fall apart on me between these trembling hands! . . . You understand," he continued in a drier, more matter-of-fact tone, "as the situation has turned out, your remaining in the monastery can no longer continue. It is in fact canonical, isn't it, my son, that a monk whose father is terminally ill or becomes impoverished is given leave by his Prior to build up his patrimony and succor the author of his days. I, however, need you even more urgently. Your brother and nephews are gone, and now you are the one who carries the life torch of our house! You are a flame which I kindled, and I cannot tolerate that it should gutter out and disappear in a cell. Know one thing" – he had read in the warm brown eyes a genuine sympathy, and the deferential demeanor of the monk seemed to promise a blind obedience – "I am sicker than you imagine. Isn't that so, Isaschar?" He turned around towards a slender figure who had quietly approached the chair of the old man from a side door with a small flask and a spoon, and who now was nodding assent with his pale head. "I am on my way thither, but I tell you Astorre: if you do not grant my wish, then your father will refuse to board the barge of the grim reaper and I will remain sitting huddled on the twilit shore!"

The monk gently stroked the fevered hand of the old man, but with conviction answered two words: "My vows!"

Ezzelino unrolled the papal letter.

"Your vows?" wheedled the old Vicedomini, "Loose cords! Chains filed through! Just move and they fall away. The holy Church, to which you owe reverence and obedience, declares them void and of no effect. There it is written." His gaunt finger pointed to the parchment with the papal seal.

The monk approached the ruler deferentially, took the writing and read it, as four eyes observed him. Reeling, he took a step back, as if he were standing on a high tower and saw the land below him suddenly disappear.

Ezzelino supported the swaying man under the arm with the concise question: "To whom did you give your vows, monk? yourself? or the Church?"

"Naturally both," screamed the old man, incensed. "That is damned splitting of hairs. Watch out for that man, my son! He intends to bring us Vicedominis to beggary."

Without anger, Ezzelino put his right hand on his beard and vowed, "Should Vicedomini die, the monk here, his son, shall inherit from him and shall endow – if the family dies out with him and if he loves me and the city of his birth – a hospital of such an extent and magnificence that the hundred cities" – he meant the cities of Italy – "shall envy us. Now, old father, that I have cleared myself of the charge of rapacity, may I direct a couple of other questions to the monk? You permit me?"

At this the old man was gripped with such wrath that he fell into convulsions. Still, he did not let go of the monk's arm, which he had again taken hold of.

Isaschar cautiously brought a spoon completely filled with a strong-smelling essence close to the pale lips. The tortured old man turned his head away with an effort . "Leave me alone!" he groaned. "You are also the governor's doctor!" and he closed his eyes.

The Jew turned his eyes, which were gleaming black and very intelligent, toward the tyrant, as if he were begging forgiveness for this distrustfulness.

"Will he return to consciousness?" asked Ezzelino.

"I believe so," replied the Jew. "He is still alive and will awaken again, but not for long, I'm afraid. He will not see the setting of today's sun."

The tyrant seized the moment to speak with Astorre, who was busied about his unconscious father.

"A word with you, monk!" said Ezzelino and ran the outspread fingers of his right hand – his favorite gesture – through the curls of his beard. "How much did the three vows which you swore some ten and more years ago, I am guessing you are about thirty," – the monk nodded – "cost you?"

Astorre cast up his clear eyes and replied without deliberation, "Poverty and obedience, nothing. I am not interested in wealth and find it easy to obey." He paused and blushed.

The tyrant found delight in this masculine abstention. Changing the subject, "Did this one cajole you into your position or force it on you?"

"No," declared the monk. "for a long time, according to family history, in our family the last of three or four sons becomes a cleric; it may be so that we Vicedominis have an intercessor, or to safeguard the inheritance and the family's power – whatever, the custom is old and honorable. I knew my lot, which was not repugnant to me, from my youth. No compulsion was used on me."

"And the third?" concluded Ezzelino – he meant the third vow. Astorre understood him.

With a renewed, but less noticeable blushing, he replied, "It has not been easy for me, but I have been able to manage it like other monks, when they are well advised – and I was so. By St. Anthony," he added reverently.

This meritorious saint, as you know, ladies and gentlemen, lived for several years with the Franciscans in Padua," explained Dante.

"How should we not know?" joked one of the listeners. "Haven't we venerated the relic which swims around in that pond in the monastery: I mean the pike which attended the sermon of the saint, converted, gave up eating flesh, persevered in righteousness and even now at a great age as a strict vegetarian – " he swallowed the end of his joke when Dante frowned at him.

"And what did he advise you?" asked Ezzelino?

"To embrace my position, for better or worse," reported the monk, "as an exacting duty, somewhat like military service, which indeed also demands obedient muscles, and deprivations which a valiant soldier should not even feel as such: to till the earth by the sweat of my brow, to eat in moderation, fast in moderation, to receive confession from neither girls nor young women, to walk in the sight of God and not worship his mother more fervently than the breviary prescribes."

The tyrant smiled. Then he stretched out his right hand toward the monk, in exhortation or blessing, and spoke, "Happy fellow! You have a lucky star! Your today arises easily from your yesterday and becomes all of a sudden your tomorrow! You are something, and not a trifle: you exercise the office of compassion, the worth of which I admit, even though I hold a different one. If you were to enter the world, which follows its own set of rules, which it is too late for you to learn, then your clear star of destiny would become an *ignis fatuus*, and after a couple of silly escapades, would burst, hissing, under the derision of heaven.

"One more thing, and this I tell you as that which I am: the ruler of Padua. Your transformation was an edification to my people, an example of renunciation. The poorest consoled himself by you, whom he saw sharing his meager food and hard toil. If you throw the frock away, if you, a high-born man, marry a high-born woman, if you scoop with both hands out of the treasures of your house, then you would rob the people who had taken possession of you as an equal in property, you make me unhappy and unsatisfied, and if anger, disobedience, indignation, should arise from it, I wouldn't wonder. One thing follows another!"

"I and Padua cannot do without you! With your handsome and gallant figure the crowd notices you and you also have more, or at least a nobler, spirit than your uncouth brothers. When the people in their raging manner seek to murder this one – he pointed to Isaschar – because he brings them assistance, which nearly happened – it lacked but little – during the last plague, who will defend him, like you did, against the crazed mob, until I arrive and put a stop to it?"

"Isaschar, help me persuade the monk!" Ezzelino turned to the medicine man with a savage smile. "For your sake, if nothing else, he should not be allowed to forsake the frock."

"Master," whispered the latter, "under your scepter the brutish scene which you punished as justly as you did bloodily, will hardly recur, and as far as I am concerned, whose faith values the continuation of the family line as God's greatest blessing, the noble one" – already in such terms and no longer as the revered one did he refer to the monk – "cannot remain unmarried."

Ezzelino smiled at the delicacy of the Jew. "And whither are your thoughts tending, monk?" he asked.

"They stand and persevere! Yet I would that – God forgive me the sin – father should not wake again, so that I will not have to oppose him! If he had only received the last rites!" He violently kissed the cheeks of the unconscious man, who thereupon regained consciousness.

The revived man sighed deeply, lifted his heavy eyelids and directed from below the grey bushiness of his shaggy eyebrows a look of supplication to the monk. "How does it stand?" he asked. "To what have you sentenced me, beloved? Heaven or hell?"

"Father," pleaded Astorre in an agitated voice, "your time is up! Your hour has arrived! Put away worldly things and cares! Think about your soul! Look, your priests" – he meant those of the parish church – "are gathered in the next room and are waiting with the sacrament of extreme unction."

And so it was. The door of the adjacent chamber was gingerly opened, a soft candle light glimmered, hardly visible in the daylight, a choir softly sang the introit, and the quiet ringing of a small bell became audible.

Now the old man, already feeling his knees sink into the cold current of the Lethe, grabbed onto the monk, as once Saint Peter on the Sea of Galilee had the Savior. "You will do it for me!" His speech was slurred.

"If I could! If I were permitted!" sighed the monk. "By all that is holy, father, think of eternity! Let go of what is earthly! Your hour has arrived!"

This veiled refusal kindled the last life of old Vicedomini into a blazing flame. "Disobedient! Ingrate!" he said in anger.

Astorre motioned to the priests.

"By all the devils," raged the old man, "leave me in peace with your jawing and silly talk! I have nothing to lose, I am already accursed and will remain so even in the midst of the heavenly cotillion, if my son willfully goes against me and ruins the essence of my life."

The appalled monk, deeply shaken by this horrific blaspheming, saw his father irretrievably falling into eternal damnation. That's what he thought, and he was firmly convinced of it, as I would have been in his place. In dark desperation he fell to his knees before the dying man and begged him with a torrent of tears, "Sir, I implore you, have pity on yourself and on me!"

"Let the sly dog be on his way!" murmured the tyrant. The monk did not hear.

Again he gave the astonished priests a sign, and the last rites were about to begin.

But the old man scrunched up in a ball like a defiant child and shook his grey head.

"Let the cunning dog go the way he wants to," urged Ezzelino more loudly.

"Father, Father!" sobbed the monk, and his heart melted in compassion.

"Noble Sir and Christian brother," a priest now asked in an uncertain voice, "are you in a condition to receive your Creator and Savior?" The old man said nothing.

"Do you stand firm in the belief on the holy trinity? Answer me, Sir!" asked the cleric a second time and became pale as a sheet, for: "Be it denied and blasphemed!" called out the dying man in a strong voice, "blasphemed and –"

"No more!" cried the monk and sprang to his feet. "I will do as you wish, Sir! Do with me as you will! Just do not plunge yourself into the flames."

The old man sighed as if he had just completed a great exertion. Then he looked around, relieved, I almost had said, pleased. He took fumbling hold of Diana's shock of blond hair, drew the woman up from her knees, took her hand, which did not refuse, opened the monk's fist and joined the two.

"Valid! in the presence of the most holy sacrament!" he exulted, and blessed the pair. The monk did not object, and Diana closed her eyes.

"Now quick, reverend fathers!" urged the old man, "it must needs hurry, as it appears to me, and I am in a Christian condition."

The monk and his bride wanted to withdraw behind the throng of priests. "Stay," murmured the dying man, "stay that my comforted eyes may see you together until they give out!" Astorre and Diana, barely moving a few steps back, had to stand with joined hands before the expiring stare of the persistent old man.

The latter mumbled a short confession, received the last rites and departed, while they anointed his soles and the priest pronounced that magnificent "Fly up, Christian soul!" The dead face wore the unmistakable expression of triumphant cunning.

The tyrant had, while all around him were on their knees, regarded the holy proceeding sitting down and with quiet attention, something like one would observe a foreign custom or like a scholar would view a sacrifice depicted on the sarcophagus of an ancient people. He approached the dead man and closed his eyes.

Then he turned to Diana. "My lady," he said, "I think we should take you home. Your parents, even if informed of your rescue, will want to see you. Also, you are wearing a dress of inferiors, which suits you not."

"Prince, I thank you and will follow you," returned Diana, but she let her hand rest in that of the monk, whose glance she until now had avoided. Now she looked full in the face of her husband and spoke with a deep, but pleasant-sounding voice, while her cheeks darkened attractively: "My lord and master, we could not have let the soul of your father perish. So I became yours. Preserve towards me better faithfulness than to the monastery. Your brother did not love me. Forgive me for speaking so: I am saying the simple truth. You will possess in me a good and obedient wife. But I have two traits which you must beware of. I am hot-tempered when anyone infringes right or honor by me, and I am therein punctilious that no one should promise me something without fulfilling it. Even as a child I tolerated that ill or not at all. I have few wants and demand nothing beyond the ordinary; only where something has been shown and promised to me, must I have the fulfillment, otherwise I lose faith and become more mortified than other women do over injustice. But how can I speak so to you, my lord and master, whom I hardly know. Farewell, my husband, and give me nine days to mourn your brother." Then she slowly withdrew her hand and disappeared with the tyrant.

In the meantime, the ecclesiastical throng had removed the body to lay it out on a bier in the chapel of the house and consecrate it.

Astorre stood alone in his discarded monk's garb which covered a breast filled with regret. An army of servants who had overheard and sufficiently understood the strange scene, approached their new master in servile attitudes and with timid gestures, bewildered and awed less by the change in masters than by the supposed sacrilege of the broken vows – the softly read letter did not reach their ears – and by the worldly conversion of the venerated monk. The latter found himself unable to mourn his father. It dawned on him now, when he was again master of his will, the suspicion – what am I saying – the revolting certainty came over him that a dying man had betrayed his good faith and abused his compassion. He discovered in the despair of the old man the den of cunning and in the frenzied blasphemy a calculated gamble at the threshold of death. Reluctantly, almost hostilely, his thoughts turned to the wife he had inherited. The convoluted monkish notion occurred to him, not to love her from his own heart, but rather solely as a representative of his dead brother; but his better sense and honest disposition rejected the shameful subterfuge. Since he now regarded her as his own, he could not avoid a certain astonishment than she had addressed him with such a peremptory speech and uncompromising frankness and had confronted him so matter-of-factly, without beating around the bush, a much more earthy and real figure than the delicate apparitions of legend. He had thought women to be softer.

The monk now became aware of his habit and the contrariety to it of his feelings and reflections. He was ashamed of his frock, and it became burdensome to him. "Give me some worldly clothes!" he ordered. Bustling servants surrounded him, from which he soon emerged in the costume of his drowned brother, with whom he shared about the same build.

At the same instant, the jester of his father, Gocciola by name, threw himself at his feet and paid homage to him, not, like the others, to request an extension of his service, but his departure and permission to change his position, for he was weary of the world, his hair was turning gray, and it suited him ill to go into eternity with a tinkling fool's cap. With these whiney words he took possession of the discarded frock, which the servants had been afraid to touch. But his checkered brain did a somersault and he added lasciviously, "I'd like to eat amarellas once more before I say farewell to the world and its deceptions. A wedding around here is not far off, I bet." He licked his chops with his sallow tongue. Then he bent the knee to the monk, shook his bells, and sprang away, dragging the frock after him.

"Amarellas or Amare," explained Dante, "is what the wedding pastry of Padua was called on account of its bitter almond taste, as well as with a delicate hint at the verb of the first conjugation.   Here the storyteller paused and shaded his forehead and eyes with his hand, considering the further course of his tale.

Meanwhile. the prince's majordomo, an Alsatian by the name of Burcardo, with measured steps, elaborate obeisances, and extensive apologies that he had to disturb the conversation, appeared before Cangrande, from whom he sought orders concerning some household matter. Germans were at that time no rare sight at the Ghibelline[3] courts of Italy; indeed they were sought after and preferred over the natives on account of their probity and their inborn sense for ceremonies and customs.

When Dante again raised his head, he became aware of the Alsatian and heard his foreign speech constantly alternating between soft and harsh, which amused the court, but sorely offended the delicate ear of the poet. His gaze then rested with obvious pleasure on the two youths, Ascanio and the armored warrior. At the last, he let his gaze rest musingly on the two women, the princess Diana, who had perked up and whose marble cheeks had become tinged with red, and Antiope,

---

[3]   Referring to the aristocratic party in medieval Italy and Germany that supported the claims of the German emperors against the papacy. [Translator's footnote]

Candgrade's lady friend, a comely and artless being. Then he continued.

Behind the Vicedomini's city castle there used to be – now that the illustrious family has died out long ago the place is completely different – a large area stretching up to the foot of the solid and thick city walls, so extensive that it contained pasture for flocks, enclosures for bucks and does, ponds filled with fish, dark woods and sunny grape arbors. One bright morning, seven days after the funeral, the monk Astorre sat in the black shadow of a cedar, leaning against the trunk and stretching the points of his shoes out into the burning sunlight. He kept this name among the Paduans, notwithstanding that he had become worldly, during his brief passage upon the earth. He sat across from a fountain which sprayed a cool stream from the mouth of an apathetic mask, not far from a stone bench, to which he had preferred the soft cushion of the rising greensward.

While he was pondering or dreaming, I know not which, two young men suddenly appeared on the piazza in front of the palace, by now lit by the almost midday sun. They were on dust-covered horses, the one armored, the other choicely dressed, albeit in traveling garb. Ascanio and Germano, as the riders were called, were the protégés of the governor and likewise the boyhood playmates of the monk, with whom he had learned and played as brothers until his fifteenth year, the start of his novitiate. Ezzelino had sent them to his father-in-law, Emperor Frederick.

Dante paused and bowed to the great shadow.

Their commissions answered, they were returning to the tyrant, to whom they also brought the new thing of the day: a copy, prepared in the imperial chancellery, of a pastoral letter to the Christian clergy, in which, before the whole world, the Holy Father accuses the brilliant emperor of extreme impiety.

Despite having been entrusted with important, perhaps extremely urgent, commissions, and the document burdened with mischief, the two could not refrain from stopping by the home of their boyhood playmate on their way to the tyrant's municipal hall. At the last hostel before they reached Padua, where without neglecting their duty they had fed and watered their horses, they had learned from the garrulous innkeeper of Padua's great misfortune and even greater vexation, the sinking of the wedding boat and the discarded frock of the monk, with apparently all the surrounding circumstances, excluding, however, the betrothal of Diana and Astorre, which had not been made public. The indissoluble bonds which tie us to the playmates of our childhood! Touched by the extraordinary fate of Astorre, the two could not rest until with their own eyes they had seen him who had been recovered. For years they had met the monk only occasionally in the street, greeting him with a friendly, but out of genuine reverence, a severe and somewhat distant, nod of the head.

Gocciola, whom they found in the courtyard of the palace. as he was busy with a roll while sitting on a small wall with his legs dangling, led them into the garden. Walking on ahead of them, the Fool conversed with the young men, not about the tragic fate of the house, but about his own affairs, which appeared to him far more important. He told them that he was striving ardently toward his blessed end, and in the telling he swallowed what was left of his roll, without having chewed it with his wobbly teeth, so that he nearly choked. Ascanio broke out into such laughter over the faces that Gocciola made and over his yearning for a monastic cell that he would have cleared the clouds from the heavens, if they had not already luxuriated in glowing colors from their own joy.

Ascanio allowed himself to tease the simpleton, not the less in order to get rid of the annoying escort. "You poor fellow," he began, "you'll never reach a cell, because, between us, in strictest confidence, my uncle, the tyrant, has cast a covetous eye upon you. Let me tell you: he has four fools, the Stoic, the Epicurean, the Platonist, and the Sceptic, as he calls them. When he is in a grave mood and wants diversion, these four stand at his beck, each in one corner of a room, on the vaulted ceiling of which the stars of the sky and the planets are depicted. My uncle, dressed in a house frock, stands in the middle of the room, claps his hands, and the philosophers hop from one corner to the next. Day before yesterday, the Stoic was howling and whining because being insatiable, he had swallowed several pounds of noodles at once. My uncle hinted to me in passing, he was of a mind to replace him, and would request you, O Gocciola, from the monk, your new master, as an inheritance tax. That's how matters stand. Ezzelino is looking for you. Who knows whether he isn't right behind you." This was a reference to the omnipresence of the tyrant which kept the Paduans in fear and constant trembling. Gocciola let out a cry as if the hand of the powerful one fell on his shoulder, and even though no one was behind him besides his short shadow, he fled with chattering teeth into some hiding place.

"I retract Ezzelino's fools." Dante interrupted himself with a pen-holding gesture, as if he were writing his tale, rather than telling it, as he was doing. "The trait is untrue, or then Ascanio was lying. It is completely unthinkable that such a serious and originally noble spirit as Ezzelino would have fed fools and enjoyed their nonsense." Dante aimed this direct thrust at his host, upon whose cloak sat Gocciola, grinning at the poet.

Cangrande was not grinning. He promised himself quietly to pay it back with interest at the first opportunity.

Satisfied, almost buoyant, Dante continued his tale.

At last the two discovered the un-monked monk, who, as I said, was leaning back against the trunk of a pine --"

"Against the trunk of a cedar, Dante," corrected the princess, who had begun to pay attention.

"– of a cedar and was sunning his toes. He did not notice the two young men approaching him from both sides, so deep was he lost in his empty or crowded dreams. Now the mischievous Ascanio bent over to pluck a grass stem and tickled the monk's nose, so that he sneezed three powerful sneezes. Astorre in friendliness gripped the hands of his boyhood pals and drew them down next to him on the turf. "So, what do you think?" he asked, in a tone that sounded rather bashful than intending to invite conversation.

"First of all, my sincere praise to your prior and your monastery," joked Ascanio. "They have preserved you well. You look younger than either of us. Of course, the close-fitting worldly dress and the clean-shaven chin might also make you look younger. Do you know, you are a handsome man? You are lying under this immense cedar just like the first man, whom God, as those who are learned maintain, created as a thirty year old, and I," he continued with an innocent expression, since he saw the monk reddening over his jesting, "am truly the last one to criticize you for freeing yourself of the frock, for the preservation of the species is the desire of everything living."

"It was not my desire, nor my free decision," confessed the monk truthfully. "Reluctantly I conformed to the will of a dying father."

"Really," smiled Ascanio. "Do not tell anyone that, Astorre, besides us who love you. Others would count this lack of independence as ridiculous or even despicable. And, speaking of the ridiculous, be careful, I beg of you, Astorre, to develop the man out of the monk without offending against good taste! The delicate transition should be carefully graduated and protected. Take some advice! Travel for a year, for example to the Court of the Emperor, from which the messengers never cease to run back and forth to Padua. Get Ezzelino to send you to Palermo! There you will learn in the company of the most accomplished knights and the most open-minded people – I mean our second Frederick – and get to know women and rid yourself of the monastic conceits of idolizing or denigrating them. The temper of the ruler colors the court and the city. The way life here in Padua under my uncle, the tyrant, has become, barbarous, extravagant, and violent, gives you a false picture of the world. Palermo, where play and earnestness, virtue and vice, fidelity and inconstancy are mixed together in their proper proportions under the most humane of all rulers, offers a truer picture. There you would fritter away the course of a year with our lady friends and foewomen in a correct or a lax manner" – the monk frowned – "you might participate in a campaign – without however, rashly exposing yourself – think of your destiny – just enough so that you remember how to handle a horse and a sword – as a boy you understood that – keep your lively brown eyes, which – by the torch of Aurora! – gleam and sparkle since you have left the monastery, open in all directions and return to us a man who is master of himself and others."

"He'll have to marry a Swabian there at the Emperor's," advised the armored one good-naturedly. "They are more devout and dependable than our women."

"Will you be quiet!" Ascanio threatened him with his finger. "Don't bore me with straw blond pigtails!" But the monk squeezed Germano's right hand, of which he had not let go.

"Seriously, Germano," he inquired, "what do you think of it?"

"Of what?" asked the latter gruffly.

"Of my new status?"

"Astorre, my friend," answered the mustachioed one somewhat embarrassed, "it is done, one doesn't thereafter ask around for advice and opinion. You take your stand where you are. But if you are dead set on knowing my opinion, well, look, Astorre, breach of trust, broken word, desertion, and the like, one gives these things harsh names in Germany. Naturally in your case it is somewhat different, you can't really compare – and then the dying father – Astorre, my dear friend, you have handled things quite prettily, only, the opposite course would have been even prettier. That's my opinion," he concluded ingenuously.

"So you would have, if you had been there, denied me the hand of your sister, Germano?"

This fell like a bolt from the blue. "The hand of my sister? Diana? the same one who is in mourning for your brother?"

"The same. She is my betrothed."

"Oh splendid!" now cried the worldly wise Ascanio, and "Wonderful!" Germano added his approbation. "Let me embrace you, brother-in-law!" The armored one, despite his forthrightness, had good breeding. But he repressed a sigh. As sincerely as he esteemed his austere sister, he would, according to his natural feelings, have given the monk, as he sat next to him, another woman.

So he twirled his mustache, and Ascanio turned the conversation. "Actually, Astorre," said the latter jovially, "we should begin by getting to know one another again; not fewer than your fifteen years of contemplative monastic life lie between our childhood and today. Not that we have in the mean time changed our character – who changes that? But we have grown up. This one for example" – he pointed to Germano – "now enjoys a fine reputation for skill with weapons; but I have this to complain of him, that he has become half German. He . . ." Ascanio bent his arm as if emptying a stein, "and then becomes sunk in thought or quarrelsome. He also scorns our lovely Italian. 'I will speak German with you,' he brags, and growls out the bear-like noises of an inhuman language. Then his servants turn pale, his creditors flee, and our Paduan women turn their handsome backs on him. In such a way he has perhaps remained as virginal as you, Astorre," and he laid his hand on the monk's shoulder in an intimate gesture.

Germano laughed heartily and replied, pointing to Ascanio, "And this one here has found his calling in that he has become the perfect courtier."

"You are mistaken there, Germano," replied the favorite of Ezzelino. "My calling was to take life easy and live merrily." And as a proof of this he called over in a friendly manner the child of the gardener, whom he had spied in the distance stealing up and peering at her new master, the monk. The pretty thing was carrying on her laughing head a basket overflowing with grapes and figs and appeared rather impish than bashful. Ascanio had jumped up. He put his left hand around the slender waist of the girl and with his right picked a grape out of the basket. At the same time, his mouth sought the swelling lips. "I'm thirsty," he said. The girl was discomfited, but stood still because she did not want to spill her fruit. Displeased, the monk turned away from the two flirts, and the dismayed girl ran away, having seen the severe monkish gesture, bestrewing her path with rolling fruits. Ascanio, who held his grapes in his hand, picked up two other bunches behind the fleeting steps, one of which he offered to Germano, who, however, threw the unfermented grapes contemptuously in the grass. The other he handed to the monk, who likewise left it untouched for a while, but then absent-mindedly tasted a juicy berry, and then soon a second, and a third.

"A courtier?" continued Ascanio, who, amused by the prudishness of the thirty-year old monk, had thrown himself back down on the grass next to him. "Don't believe it, Astorre! Believe the opposite! I am the only one who gently, but clearly, encourages my uncle not to become cruel-hearted, but to remain a human being."

"He is only righteous and true to himself!" put in Germano.

"As respects his justice!" complained Ascanio, "and as respects his logic! Padua is an imperial fiefdom.

Ezzelino is governor. Whoever displeases him, rebels against the Empire. Those who commit high treason get – " he could not bring himself to utter the words. "Horrible," he murmured. "And anyway, why can't we Italians lead a life of our own under our warm sun? why this hazy phantasm of the Empire which stifles our breath? I am not speaking for me. I am chained to my uncle. If the emperor, may God preserve him, should die, then all of Italy will throw itself with curses and maledictions against the tyrant Ezzelino, and they'll strangle the nephew merely in passing." Ascanio looked at the gleaming heaven above the lush earth and sighed.

"That makes two of us," added Germano cold-bloodedly. "That, however, can wait. The master has a confirmed prophesy. The learned Guido Bonatti and Paul of Bagdad, who with his long beard sweeps up the dust in the street, have puzzled out for him a new horoscope in agreement with each other, notwithstanding how much those mutually jealous men usually contradict each other. It is as follows: sooner or later a son of the peninsula will win the undivided crown of the peninsula with the help of a German emperor, who for his part north of the mountains will meld together everything German into one solid empire. Is Frederick the emperor? Is the king Ezzelino? Only God, who knows the day and the hour, can tell, but the master has wagered his glory and our lives on it!"

"A tangle of sense and craziness!" Ascanio was irritated; while the monk was astonished at the power of the stars, the fulsome ambition of the ruler and the stream of the world which pulled everything with it. Too, he was appalled at the specter of the incipient cruelty of Ezzelino, in whom the innocent young man had seen the embodiment of justice.

Ascanio answered his unexpressed doubts as he continued: "Let them both die an evil death, Guido of the furrowed brow and the bearded heathen! They cozen my uncle into following his whims and inclinations while he thinks he is doing what is necessary. Have you observed him, Germano, at his meager repast as he colors the water in the transparent crystal of his goblet with the three or four blood-red drops of wine which he allows himself? as his alert gaze follows the blood which slowly disperses and diffuses throughout the pure water? or how he loves to close the eyes of the dead so that it has become an act of courtesy to invite the governor to a solemnization at the deathbed and allow him to perform this sad duty? Ezzelino, my prince, do not become gruesome to me!" cried the young man, overpowered by his feelings.

"I think not, nephew," said a voice behind him. It was Ezzelino, who had approached unseen and, though no eavesdropper, had heard the last painful outcry of Ascanio.

The three young men quickly stood up and greeted the sovereign, who sat down on the bench. His countenance was as impassive as the mask of the fountain.

"You my messengers," he took Ascanio and Germano to task, "what came over you that you visited this one" he nodded subtly toward the monk, "before me?"

"He is our boyhood playmate and has experienced something unusual." The nephew made excuse, and Ezzelino accepted it. He received the correspondence which Ascanio, bending the knee, handed him. He stuffed everything in his breast pocket except the Bull. "See here," he said. "The latest. Read it aloud, Ascanio! You have younger eyes than I."

Ascanio read the apostolic letter aloud, while Ezzelino buried his right hand in his beard and listened with demonic pleasure.

First the triple-crowned author gave the quick-witted Emperor the name of an apocalyptic monster. "I am familiar with that; it is absurd," said the tyrant. "The Pontiff has also referred to me intemperately in his letters until I warned him to chastise to me, who am called Ezzelino the Roman, in the future in classical language. How does he refer to me this time? I'm curious. Find the place, Ascanio – I'm sure there is one – where he reproaches me with the evil doings of my father-in-law. Give it here!" He grabbed the letter and soon found the place: here the Pope accused the

Emperor of loving the husband of his daughter, "Ezzelino da Romano, the worst criminal in the inhabited world."

"Correct!" praised Ezzelino, and gave the writing back to Ascanio. "Read me the impieties of the Emperor, nephew," he smiled.

Ascanio read that Frederick had said that alongside much delusion, there were only two true gods: nature and reason. The tyrant shrugged his shoulders.

Ascanio read further that Frederick had said: three imposters, Moses, Mohammed, and – he faltered – had deceived the world. "Superficial," criticized Ezzelino. "They had their stars; but, whether it was said or not, the sentiment sinks in and counts as much as an army and a fleet for the one wearing the tiara. Continue."
Now there came a bizarre tale. Frederick, riding through a waving field of grain, was joking with his retinue and in a blasphemous reference to the sacred Host sang out this triplet:

As rife as heads of grain are deities,
They shoot up rapidly in the sun
And they wave their golden heads in the breeze –

Ezzelino thought for a moment. "Strange!" he whispered. "My memory has retained this little verse. It is absolutely authentic. The emperor called it out to me with a happy, laughing mouth, as close by the ruins of the temple of Enna, we rode together through those bountiful grain fields with which the goddess Ceres blessed Sicilain soil. I can recall it with the same clarity which sparkled over the island on that summer day. I am not the one who imparted this genial witticism to the Pontiff. I am too serious for such a thing. Who did it? I'll make you judges, youngsters. Three of us were riding, and the third – I am as sure of it as I am of this shining sun " – the sun just then threw a ray through the leaves – "was Peter de Vinca, the inseparable companion of the emperor. Was perchance the pious chancellor fearful for his soul and has relieved his conscience by a letter to Rome? Is a Saracen riding today? Yes? Quick, Ascanio. I shall dictate a few lines."

The latter brought forth a tablet and pen, knelt on his right knee and wrote, using his bent leg arm as a desk:

Illustrious sir and dear father-in-law: A quick word. The little verse in the Bull – you are too rich in invention to repeat yourself – was heard by only four ears, mine and those of your Peter, in the grainfield of Enna, a year ago, when you called me to your court and I rode over the island with you. No rooster would crow about it, unless it be the one of the Gospel which confirmed the betrayal of Peter. If you love me and yourself, Sir, then test your chancellor with a sharp question!"

"Bloody wordplay! I cannot write that! My hand trembles!" cried Ascanio, turning pale. "I shan't bring the chancellor to the rack!" and he threw the pen away.

"Duty," remarked Germano coolly, picked up the pen and completed the letter which he stowed under his visor. "It will travel yet today," he said. "Myself personally, I never liked the man from Capua: he has shifty eyes."

The monk Astorre shivered despite the midday sun. For the first time the man who had come out of the cloister grasped with both hands the distrustfulness or the betrayal in the world, as if they were the slithery coils of an adder. Astorre was recalled from his brooding by a stern word from Ezzelino which, as the latter was getting up from the stone bench, he directed to the monk.

"Tell me, monk, why do you bury yourself in your house? You have not left it once since you put on worldly clothing. Are you afraid of public opinion? Confront it! It will shrink back. But if you make a move to flight, then it will fasten onto your heel like a howling mob. Have you visited your fiancée Diana? The week of mourning is over. I advise you: invite your relatives today, and marry Diana before the day is over!"

"And then quickly betake yourselves to your remotest palace," concluded Ascanio.

"That I do not advise," forbad the tyrant. "No fear. No flight. Today you marry, and tomorrow you hold a masked reception. Good bye." He departed, motioning Germano to follow him.

"May I interrupt," asked Cangrade, who was polite enough to wait for a natural pause in the story.

"You are the master," returned the Florentine sullenly.

"Do you believe that the immortal emperor really said that about the three great impostors?"

"It is not clear."

"I mean in your heart of hearts."

Dante answered in the negative with a decisive shake of his head.

"And still you have damned him as an atheist in the sixth circle of your hell. How could you do that? Justify yourself!"

"Majesty," answered the Florentine, "the Comedy speaks to the age in which I live. And this age justly or unjustly reads the most horrible blasphemies on that noble forehead. I can do nothing against pious opinion. Perhaps posterity will judge otherwise."

"My Dante," asked Cangrande again, "do you believe Peter de Vinca innocent of the betrayal of the Emperor and the Empire?"

"It is not clear."

"I mean in your heart of hearts."

Dante answered in the negative with the same gesture.

"And you let the traitor maintain his innocence in your Comedy?"

"Lord," Dante justified himself, "where clear proofs are lacking, am I to accuse a son of the peninsula the more of treason because there are so many disingenuous and equivocal men amongst us?"

"Dante, my Dante," said the prince, "you don't believe a man is guilty, and you damn! You believe a man is guilty, and you pardon!" Then he continued the story in a playful frolic:

"The monk and Ascanio now also left the garden and entered the hall." But Dante took over.

Not at all; rather, they climbed up into a small room in a tower, the same one that Astorre lived in as a boy with unshorn hair: for he avoided the grand and ostentatious rooms which he had yet to get used to considering as his possessions, just as he had not yet touched any of the golden hoard which had been left to him. At a commanding gesture from Ascanio the majordomo Burcardo, with a constrained gait and a sullen expression, followed them both at a measured distance.

Cangrande's steward of the same name had come back into the room after taking care of some errands, and was listening with curiosity since he had noticed that the story involved well-known persons; when he heard himself named and saw himself suddenly in the mirror of the story as large as life he found this abuse of the honor of his person audacious and utterly improper in the mouth of the scholar and refugee who was being tolerated and given accommodations in the house, for whom he had, in a just consideration of the circumstances and differences, prepared the simplest room imaginable in the upper part of the prince's house. What the others suffered with a smile, he took as an irritant. He furrowed his brow and rolled his eyes. With a serious countenance the Florentine delighted in the indignation of the prissy man and continued with his story.

"Worthy sir," began Ascanio to the majordomo – did I mention that the latter by birth was an Alsatian? – "how does one marry in Padua? Astorre and I are inexperienced children in this science."

The steward assumed a pose, staring fixedly at his master, without bestowing a glance at Ascanio, who, according to his notion had no business giving him any orders.

"Distinguendum est," he said solemnly. "Things should be kept separate: the courtship, the wedding, the reception."

"Where is that written?" jested Ascanio.

"Ecce!" answered the majordomo, opening a large book which never left him. "Here!" and he pointed to the title with the outstretched finger of his left hand. It read: "The Ceremonies of Padua According to Close Investigation, for the Use and Benefit of all Decent and Respectable Persons, Compiled by Mister Godoscalco Burcardo." He turned the page and read, "Section One: The Courtship. Paragraph One: The serious suitor brings along a friend of equal standing as a valid witness –"

"By the abundant blessings of my patron saint!" Ascanio interrupted him impatiently. "Leave us in peace with ante and post, with courtship and reception, give us the middle piece: how does one marry in Padua?"

"In Batova," cawed the piqued Alsatian, whose barbaric accent was more prominent than usual when he was upset, "the twelve leading families are invited to the solemnization of the nuptials" – he named them from memory – "ten days in advance, not sooner, not later, by the majordomo of the groom, accompanied by six servants. In this illustrious gathering the rings are exchanged. One sips Cyprian wine and as wedding pastries amarellas are eaten."

"Pray God that we don't break our teeth on them!" Ascanio laughed, and grabbing the book from the majordomo, read through the names, of which six heads of families – six of the twelve – and some young persons, were crossed out with thick lines. They probably were involved in some conspiracy against the tyrant and thereby met their demise.

"Pay attention old fellow!" commanded Ascanio, acting for the monk, who had sunk back into an upholstered chair and, being lost in thought, made no objection to the friendly patronization. "You make your rounds with your six layabouts this minute, right now, without delay, understand? and invite the guests for today at vespers."

"Ten days in advance," repeated Sr. Burcardo majestically, as if proclaiming an imperial law.

"Today, for today, mule-brain!"

"Impossible," said the majordomo serenely. "Would you change the course of the stars and the seasons?"

"Do you rebel? Is you neck itching, old fellow?" Ascanio gave warning with a strange smile.

That was sufficient. Sr. Burcardo got the message. Ezzelino had given an order, and the most obstinate sticklers complied without grumbling, so strict was the tyrant's rod.

"And you will not invite the two ladies Canossa, Olympia and Antiope."

"Why not?" asked the monk suddenly, as if touched by a magic wand. The air colored before his eyes, and an image arose, just the first outline of which captivated his whole soul.

"Because the Countess Olympia is a fool, Astorre. Don't you know the story of the poor woman? But at the time you were still in your swaddling clothes, that is to say the frock. It was three years ago, as the leaves were turning,"

"In the summer, Ascanio. It is just now a year," contradicted the monk.

"You are right – are you familiar with the story? But how could you be? At that time Count Canossa was spreading rumors among the legates, was investigated, arrested, and condemned. The Countess fell prostrate before my uncle, who wrapped himself in silence. She was then deceived in the most criminal manner by a greedy chamberlain, who, for the sake of her money claimed that the Count would be pardoned at the block. When this did not occur, and they were bringing a headless corpse to the Countess, she, being suddenly thrown from hope to despair, threw herself upon the body through a window. Miraculously she was not injured except that she sprained her ankle. But from that day on her understanding was shattered. If natural moods evolve imperceptibly from one to another like the fading daylight into the growing dusk, hers change in rapid swings from light to dark twelve times in twelve hours. Goaded by continual unease, the wretched woman hurries from her desolate town palace to her country house and from there back to town in perpetual waywardness. Today, she would marry her child off to the son of a sharecropper, because only a lowly status can secure safety and peace; tomorrow the noblest suitor, who by the way would never appear for dread of such a mother, would hardly be good enough for her –"

If Ascanio, while his words were flowing, had given the briefest glance at the monk, he would have paused in astonishment, for the countenance of the Monk was transformed by pity and compassion.

"Whenever the tyrant," he continued heedlessly, "rides by Olympia's house on the hunt, she rushes to her window and expects that he will dismount at her doorstep and take her, fallen into disfavor but now tried sufficiently, back to his court in grace and in favor, the which he truly has no desire to do. Another day, or even on the same one, she imagines to herself that she is persecuted and ostracized by Ezzelino, who does not concern himself with her. She believes herself impoverished and her goods, which he leaves untouched, confiscated. So she burns and freezes in a tertian fever of the most abrupt contradictions, is not only crazy herself, but also makes crazy whatever she draws into the whirling ambit of her mind, and causes mischief – for she is only half crazy and mixes in sayings which are witty and to the point – wherever she is believed. It is out of the question to include her in company and invite her to a celebration. It is a wonder that her child, whom she idolizes and whose marriage is in the center of her fantasy, retains her sanity upon this unstable ground. But the girl, who is in the first bloom

of youth and is tolerably pretty, is good-natured . . .."
Thus he ran on for some time.

Astorre, however, became lost in a dream. So I call it
because the past is a dream. For the monk saw what he
had experienced three years earlier: a block with the
executioner next to it and he himself as a spiritual
comforter in the place of a fellow monk who was sick;
he was waiting for a poor sinner. The latter – the Count
Canossa – appeared in chains, but absolutely refused to
cooperate, whether it was because he supposed that
now that he was at the block his pardon would not be
long in coming, or whether it was simply that he loved
the sun and abhorred the grave. He stonily ignored the
monk and spurned his prayers. An appalling struggle
ensued as he continued to balk and resist; for he held by
the hand his child, who – unnoticed by the guard – had
rushed up and grabbed onto him, making the most
expressive eyes and most imploring glances at the
monk. The father pressed the girl close to his breast
and appeared to want to protect himself from
destruction with this young life, but he was pushed
down by the executioner with his head on the block.
Thereupon the child laid her head and neck next to her
father's. Did she intend to awaken the pity of the
executioner? Did she want to embolden her father to
suffer the unavoidable? Did she want to whisper the
name of a saint in the ear of the unshriven man? Did
she do this incredible thing without thinking or

considering, out of overflowing childish love? Did she simply want to die with him?

The colors were now shining so brightly that the monk saw the two necks lying next to each other a few steps from him in their complete living reality, the brick-red neck of the count and the child's snow-white one with crinkly golden-brown downy hair. The child's neck was of the loveliest form and unusual slenderness. Astorre shuddered, the falling ax might miss its mark, and felt himself shaken in his very soul, not differently than the first time, except that he did not lose consciousness, as he did then, when the horrible scene in fact and reality took place, and he came to only after everything was over.

"Does my master have any commission to give me?" The rasping voice of the majordomo, who bore it hard to be ordered about by Ascanio, brought the monk out of his transport.

"Burcardo," answered Astorre in a soft voice, "do not forget to invite the two ladies Canossa, mother and daughter. Let it not be said that the monk distances himself from those who are avoided and abandoned by the world. I honor the right of an unfortunate" – here the majordomo agreed with eager nodding – "to be invited and received by me. Had she been passed over, it could have seriously hurt her feelings, the way she is constituted."

"On no account!" warned Ascanio. "Do not do this to yourself! Your betrothal is bizarre enough already. And the bizarre enthralls that misguided woman. She will start something unbelievable in her own way, and fling some madcap saying into the celebration which, moreover, already has all the Paduan ladies nervous and distracted."

Signore Burcardo, however, who held fast to the entitlement of a Canossa, whether in her right mind or not, to gather together with the twelve and who believed he was duty-bound to obey the Vicedomini and no other, bowed low to the monk. "Your Magnificence only will be obeyed," he said and left the room.

"Oh monk, monk!" cried Ascanio, "who carries compassion into a world that leaves hardly any good deed unpunished!"

"But the way we humans are," interposed Dante, "often a prophetic light shows us the edge of an abyss, but then comes Reason and smiles and sophisticates and talks us out of any perception of danger."

The happy-go-lucky fellow considered the matter and reassured himself in this manner: what connection on earth does that fool of a woman have with the monk, in whose life she plays not the slightest role? And after all, if she does cause laugher, she will spice up our amarellas! He was far from suspecting what was taking place in Astorre's soul, but even if he had guessed and inquired, the latter would have never disclosed his chaste secret to the worldling.

So Ascanio left the matter alone, and remembering the other command of the tyrant, to introduce the monk to society, he asked merrily, "Have you taken care of the wedding ring? For it is written in the ceremonies, section two, paragraph such-and-such: The rings are exchanged." The latter replied that there would be such a thing in the household somewhere.

"Not so, Astorre." Ascanio gave his opinion. "If you follow my advice, you will buy your Diana a new one. Who knows what history may cling to an old ring. Throw what is old behind you. It is also quite engagingly fitting: buy her a ring from the Florentine on the bridge. Do you know the man? But how could you? Listen: early this morning, returning with Germano to the city, as I was crossing our only bridge over the canal – it was so crowded that we had to dismount and lead our horses – a goldsmith, upon my word, set up his shop on the weathered top of a bridge support pillar, and all of Padua was milling around and haggling with him. Why on the narrow bridge when we have so many plazas? Because in Florence the jewelry shops are on the Arno bridge. For, – marvel at the logic of fashion! – where else do you buy fine jewelry other than from a Florentine, and where else would a Florentine display his wares if not on a bridge? He wouldn't do it any other way. Otherwise, his wares would be crude stuff and he himself no genuine Florentine. But he is, I believe. After all, he had written above his booth in giant letters: Niccolo Lippo dei Lippi the Goldsmith, driven from his homeland by a corrupt and unjust verdict, as is customary on the Arno. Come on, Astorre! Let's go to the bridge!"

The latter did not refuse, since he himself felt the need of breaking the spell of the household domain, which he had not left since he had stripped off his frock.

"Have you got money with you, friend monk?" joked Ascanio. "Your vow of poverty has expired, and the Florentine will overcharge you." He knocked at the sliding window of the household office which was in the lower hallway through which the young men were just then walking. A crafty face appeared, every line a deception, and the steward of the Vicedominis – a Genoan, if I am rightly informed – with a toadying bow handed his master a purse filled with gold byzantines. Then the monk was wrapped by a servant in the comfortable Paduan summer cloak with a hood.

In the street Astorre drew the hood down over his face, less on account of the burning rays of the sun than from habit, and turned affably to his companion. "Right, Ascanio?" he said. "I'll take care of this business alone. The purchase of a simple gold ring won't overtax my monkish wits? Of that much you will allow me to be capable? I'll see you later, at the wedding ceremony, when vespers are rung!" Ascanio went his way but called back over his shoulder, "One, not two! Diana will give you yours! Keep that in mind, Astorre!" It was one of those colorful soap bubbles of which the droll lad blew more than one a day from his lips into the air.

"If you ask me, ladies and gentlemen, why the monk let his friend go, then I say: he wanted to let the heavenly note, which the young martyr to child's love had awakened in his heart, fade away without any disturbance."

Astorre had reached the bridge which, despite the burning sun, was filled with people, and from the two riverbanks close by a double throng of people led to the shop of the Florentine. The monk remained unrecognized under his cloak, although now and again a questioning eye rested on the uncovered part of his face. Nobility and commoners sought to get ahead of one another. Elegant ladies climbed out of their sedan chairs and pushed and shoved to bargain for a pair of bangles or a headband of the latest pattern. The Florentine had caused notice to be given by crier in all the plazas that he would close shop today after the Ave Maria. He had no intention of doing so. But what does a Florentine care about a lie!

At last the monk, surrounded by people, stood at the booth. The mobbed merchant, who was making ten times his capital, looked him over with an experienced side glance and immediately recognized a neophyte. "How can I serve the educated taste of your excellency?" he asked. "Give me a simple gold ring," answered the monk. The merchant grabbed a cup, on which, after the Florentine manner and style, done in noble work, something lavish was to be seen. He shook the cup, in the belly of which a hundred rings were teeming, and offered it to Astorre.

The latter became distressingly embarrassed. He did not know the size of the finger which he was to attire with a ring, and lifting out several of them, hesitated noticeably between a large and a small one. The Florentine was unable to resist making a sarcastic comment, just as a veiled mockery runs through all discourse on the banks of the Arno. "Does the gentleman not know the size of the finger which he surely has squeezed from time to time?" he asked with an innocent expression, but as a savvy man he corrected himself immediately; and in the Florentine belief that suspicion of ignorance is insulting whereas suspicion of naughtiness is flattering, he gave Astorre two rings, one larger, and one smaller, which he adroitly passed from his thumb and forefinger to the thumb and forefinger of the monk. "For the two loves of your Excellency," he whispered, bowing.

Even before the monk could become indignant over this licentious address, he received a rough jolt. It was the shoulder blade of a horse's armor which brushed against him so rudely that he dropped the smaller ring. In the same instant the deafening sound of eight trumps blared in his ear. The music corps of the governor's German body guard rode over the bridge in two rows of four horses each, scattering all the people on the bridge and forcing them up against the stone balustrades.

As soon as the horns had passed, the monk, hiding the larger ring quickly in his clothing, dove after the smaller one, which had rolled away under the hooves of the horses.

The old structure of the bridge was worn and rutted in the middle, so that the ring rolled down the hollow and then, driven by its own momentum, up the other side. Here a young ladies' maid named Isotta, or, as they shorten it in Padua, Sotte, snatched the rolling and coruscating object, at the risk of being trampled by the horses. "A good luck ring!" exalted the simple creature and put her find, with child-like gloating, on the slender finger, the fourth of the left hand, of a young mistress whom she accompanied, inasmuch as the finger, on account of its petite form, appeared to her especially worthy of and apt for the small adornment. In Padua, however, as also here in Verona, if I am not mistaken, one wears the wedding ring on the left hand.

The young noblewoman appeared indignant over the antic of the girl, but was nevertheless somewhat amused by it. She tried vigorously to remove the strange ring, which fit her as if poured on, from her finger. Suddenly the monk was standing in front of her. He raised his arms in joyful wonder. His gesture, however, was to stretch his open right hand out before him, and raise his left hand to his heart, for he had recognized, despite her having blossomed into a young woman, from the striking slenderness of the neck, and even more from the movement of his soul, the child whose delicate head he had seen on the block.

While the young woman directed dismayed and questioning eyes at the monk and continued to twist at the recalcitrant ring, Astorre hesitated to ask for it back. But it had to be. He opened his mouth. "Young lady," he began – and felt himself enveloped by two arms in armor which seized him and lifted him into the air. In an instant he saw himself seated, with the help of another man in armor, one leg to the right, one leg to the left, on a stamping horse. "Let's see," a good-natured laughter rang out, "whether you have forgotten how to ride!" It was Germano, who rode at the head of a German cohort which he commanded, and which the governor had ordered to muster at a plain not far from Padua. Since he unexpectedly saw his friend and brother-in-law in the open, he indulged himself the innocent fun of lifting him up onto a horse next to him, which a young Swabian had vacated at a signal from him. The spirited animal, which sensed the change in riders, made a couple of wild leaps, a melee of horses ensued upon the confined bridge, and Astorre, whose hood had fallen back and who was with difficulty staying in the stirrups, was recognized by the horrified crowd which was getting out of the way. "The monk! The monk!" they called from every side, and pointed, but the martial tumult already had the bridge behind it and disappeared around a street corner. The Florentine, who had not been paid, ran after them, but hardly twenty steps, because he became uneasy about his wares left in the not-too-reliable care of a stripling, and then the calls of the crowd showed him that he was dealing with a well-known and easy-to-find personage. He asked someone to show him Astorre's palace, and called there that day, the following day, and the next day. The first two times he got nothing accomplished, because everything was topsy-turvy in the monk's household; the third time he found the seal of the tyrant on the closed gate. With this, the coward wanted nothing to do, and so he went without payment.

The women however – yet a third woman, who had been separated from Antiope and the frivolous lady's maid by the commotion on the bridge, found them again – went in the opposite direction. The third woman was a strange looking, apparently prematurely aged woman with deep furrows, a wild bush of grey hair, and an agitated visage, who dragged her neglected, but elegant dress through the dust in the middle of the street.

Sotte was just telling the old woman, apparently the mother of the young lady, with stupid exultation what happened on the bridge: Astorre – to her also the outcry of the people had disclosed his name – Astorre the monk, who, as was known throughout the city, was to marry, was, according to Sotte, to have surreptitiously rolled a golden ring to Antiope, and as she – Sotte – comprehending the gesture of providence and the slyness of the monk, put it on the dear young lady, the monk himself came up to the latter, and as Antiope out of good breeding wanted to return the ring to him, he supposedly – she imitated the monk – laid his left hand on his heart, like this! but the right hand rebuffing stretched out in a gesture that in all of Italy said nothing else than, and signified: Keep it, my love!

At last the astonished Antiope was able to speak and implore her mother to pay no attention to the stupid talk of Isotte, but in vain. Madonna Olympia raised her arms towards heaven and in the open street thanked St, Anthony with fervor that he had heard her daily prayer beyond every hope and expectation and had bestowed on her darling a virtuous man of equal rank, one of his own sons. In so doing, she gesticulated so bizarrely that the passers-by laughingly tapped their foreheads. The disconcerted Antiope made every effort imaginable to talk her mother out of the bedazzling fairy tale; but the latter did not hearken and continued passionately to build her castles in the air.

Thus the women arrived at the Canossa palace and met in the archway a stiffly decked out majordomo whom six lavishly dressed servants followed. Signore Burcardo allowed, deferentially stepping back, Madonna Olympia to ascend the steps ahead of him, then having arrived in a deserted hall, he made three bows with calculated precision, each closer and lower than the preceding one, and spoke slowly and solemnly: "Excellencies, Astorre Vicedomini sent me to invite your honorable selves most deferentially to the solemnization of his nuptials, today" – he painfully swallowed "in ten days" – "when vespers are rung."

Dante paused. His fable lay spread out in profusion before him; but his rigorous mind selected and simplified. Cangrande called to him.

"My dear Dante," he began, "I am surprised at the the hard and acidly sharp features with which you have sketched your Florentine!   Your Niccolo Lippo dei Lippi is banned by a corrupt and unjust judgment. He himself is a price gouger, a flatterer, a liar, a scoffer, a slickster and a poltroon, all 'according to the manner of the Florentines.' And that is just a tiny spark from the fiery rain of curses with which you shower your Florence, only a dribbling dreg of those bitter tercets, dripping with vinegar and gall, which you give your hometown to sample in your Comedy. Let me tell you, it is base to defame one's birthplace, to shame your mother! It is not becoming! Believe me, it makes a bad impression!"

"My dear Dante, let me tell you about a puppet show that I recently saw while wandering about among the people in disguise. You wrinkle your nose at my low taste in enjoying puppets and fools in idle moments. Nevertheless, accompany me to the front of the tiny stage. What do you see there? Man and wife are arguing. She gets a thrashing and cries. A neighbor sticks his head in the door, sermonizes, chastises, and sticks his nose in. But look! the stalwart wife stands up against the meddler and defends the husband. 'If it suits me to be thrashed,' she wails.

"Similarly, my Dante, a noble-minded person, who has been mistreated by his hometown, says, 'I want to be beaten!'"

Many young and sharp eyes were fastened on the Florentine. The latter hid his head, saying nothing. No one knew what he was thinking. When he raised it again, his brow was more careworn, his mouth bitterer, and his nose longer.

Dante listened intently. The wind howled around the corners of the castle and blew open a poorly secured shutter. Mount Baldo had sent its first snow shower. One could see the snowflakes swirling and whirling, lit up by the flames from the hearth. The poet contemplated the snowstorm; and his days, which he felt were slipping away, appeared to him in the form of this white chasing and racing through a flickering red glow. He shivered from cold.

And his sensitive listeners felt with him that no home of his own, but only the changeable favor of varying patrons sheltered him and protected him from the winter, which covered highways and byways with snow.   All became aware, and Cangrande, who possessed great spirit, first: here sits a man without a homeland!

The ruler arose, shaking the jester off his cloak like a feather, went over to the banished man, took him by the hand and led him to his own place, near the fire. "It is your due," he said, and Dante did not resist. Cangrande, however, took advantage of the vacated stool. From there he could comfortably observe the two women, between whom the wanderer through Hades sat. The firelight glowed upon him, and he continued his story thus:

While the lesser bells in Padua rang the vespers, the remainder of the twelve noble families gathered under the cedar beams of the splendorous hall of the Vicedominis, waiting for the entry of the owner. Diana stayed close by her father and brother. A soft murmur of conversation went about the room.   The men discussed seriously and thoroughly the political side of the marriage of two of the great families of the city. The young people joked in undertones about the marrying monk. The women shuddered, despite the papal letter, at the sacrilege, which only those who were surrounded by budding daughters saw in a more charitable light, excusing it by the force of circumstance, or interpreted it as proceeding from the good heart of the monk.

The presence of Olympia Canossa excited wonder and unease, for she was in striking, almost royal array, as if she were to play a major role in the pending ceremony, and she spoke of Antiope with incredible garrulousness to anyone who would listen. The latter anxiously tried, whispering and pleading, to calm down her overwrought mother. Madonna Olympia had already been mightily irritated on the steps where she – Signore Burcardo was just then busy with the reception of two other worthies – was reverentially welcomed by Gocciola, who was holding in his hand a new scarlet red cap with silver bells. Now, with the others standing in a circle, she was annoying or alarming her peers by her immoderate gesticulation. They pointed to the poor thing with winks and nods. None of them, in the monk's place, would have invited her, and everyone was prepared for her to play him one of her tricks.

Burcardo announced the master of the house. Astorre had quickly gotten away from the Germans, had hurried back to the bridge, without finding either the ring or the women, and, reproaching himself about it, although basically only chance was to be blamed, had, in the hour remaining to him until vespers, formed the resolution to act in the future always according to the rules of prudence. With this intent he entered the hall in the midst of the gathered guests. The pressure of the attention directed towards him, and the forms and claims of society, as it were, palpable in the air, made him sensible that he dare not express the reality of the situation, forceful and sometimes ugly as it is, but would have to give it an extenuating and pleasing cast. So he kept himself instinctively between truth and a fine appearance and spoke irreproachably.

"Ladies and gentlemen; fellow nobles," he began, "death has had a rich harvest among us Vicedomini. As I stand before you clothed in black, I am mourning my father, three brothers, and three nephews. That I, having been released by the Church, did not believe myself, upon serious consideration" – here the tone of his voice became muffled – "and conscientious examination, permitted to leave unfulfilled the wish of a dying father to live on in son and grandchildren, this you will judge variously, approving or condemning, according to the righteousness or clemency that inhabits your breasts. You will all agree, however, that with my history it would not have become me to hesitate and vacillate, and that in this situation only the most obvious and the unsought for could be pleasing to God. But who was nearer to me than the maiden widow of my brother, who was already united with me in the inconsolable grief over him? In such manner I grasped across a dear deathbed this hand, as I grasp it now" – he went up to Diana and led her into the middle – "and place the wedding ring on her finger." Thus he did. The ring fit. Diana did the same, in that she gave the monk a golden ring. "It is my mother's," she said, "who was a true and virtuous wife. I give you a ring which has held faithfulness. A solemnly murmured congratulations concluded the sober transaction, and the old Pizzaguerra, a dignified old man – for greed is a healthy vice and conduces to old age – cried the usual tears.

Madonna Olympia saw her dream castle burst into flames and burn with falling columns and crashing beams. She took a step forward, as if she wanted to convince her eyes that they were deceived, then a second step in growing fury, and now she stood close before Astorre and Diana, her grey hair wild and her frenzied words racing and rushing like a people in riot.

"Wretch!" she cried. "Against the ring on the finger of this person testifies another and first bestowed." She dragged Antiope forward, who had followed her in growing fear and with the most imploring gestures, and raised the hand of the girl. "This ring you placed on the finger of my child not an hour ago on the bridge by the Florentine!" So to her had a false mirror distorted the event. "Infamous man! Adulterous monk! Doesn't the earth open up to swallow you? Let the gatekeeper monk who was sleeping in intoxication and let you out of your cell, be hanged! You wanted to indulge your lusts, but you should have chosen other prey than an unjustly persecuted, helpless widow and an unprotected orphan!"

The marble flooring did not open up, and in the glances of those standing around her the unfortunate woman, who thought to have given expression to a just, maternal anger in poor and weak words, read open scorn or a pity of a different sort than she had hoped to find.   She heard behind her the distinctly audible whisper, "fool!" and her anger changed into a demented laughter.   "Oh, yes, look at the moron," she said with scornful laughter, "who could choose so stupidly between these two. I will let you be judges, gentlemen, and everyone who has eyes. Here, the lovely head, the budding youth," – and I forget the rest, but one thing I know: all the young men in the Vicedomini's hall, and more than one of them were fond of loose living, all the youth who were abstemious and those who were not, averted their eyes and ears from the scandalous words and gestures of a mother who trampled breeding and shame under foot in front of the child that she bore, and hawked her like a procuress.

Everyone in the hall felt sorry for Antiope. Only Diana, as little as she doubted the monk's fidelity, experienced I don't know what kind of vague resentment against the impudent prank played on her groom.

Antiope felt herself to blame in that she kept the unfortunate ring on her finger. Perhaps she did it so as not to aggravate her daydreaming mother, thinking that the latter would, upon being disappointed by reality, pass in her usual manner from arrogance to faintheartedness, and dismiss everything with a rolling of her eyes and a few mumbled words. Or maybe the young Antiope herself dipped her fingers in the bubbling fairytale-fountain. Was not the meeting on the bridge with the monk wondrous, and would the monk's choice of her have been more wondrous than the fate which took him out of the monastery?

Now she suffered a horrible punishment. Insofar as an unbridled speech could do so, had her own mother despoiled her of any protective mantle.

A dark red and a still darker red spread over Olympia's forehead and neck. Then, in the general silence, she began to cry loudly and bitterly.

Even the grey, eavesdropping maenads were shocked. Then a twitch of horrible pain crossed her face and her rage doubled. "And the other one," she shrieked, pointing at Diana, "this square-built piece of marble, barely hacked out of the rough! This bungled giantess, which God botched when he was still an apprentice and was learning to knead! Fie on the awkward body lacking life and soul! Who would have given her one anyway? The bastard, her mother? The stupid Orsola? Or the scrawny skinflint over there?

Only reluctantly did he give her a stingy pittance of a soul!"

The old Pizzaguerra kept calm. With the clear understanding of the greedy he did not forget whom he had before him. His daughter Diana, however, did forget it. Infuriated by the crude mocking of her body and her soul, deeply shocked, she furrowed her brow and made fists of her hands. Now that the crazy woman brought her parents into it, insulting her mother in the grave, pillorying her father, she went wild. A pale fury seized and overpowered her.

"Bitch!" she cried and punched – Antiope in the face; for the despairing and brave girl had thrown herself in front of her mother. Antiope gave a cry that shook the hall and all hearts.

Now the wheel in the foolish woman's head turned completely around. The fiercest anger subsided into unspeakable misery. "You hit my child!" she groaned, sank to her knees and sobbed, "Is there no God in heaven?"

It was the last straw. The camel's back would have broken sooner, except that the disaster took place faster than I can tell it, so fast that neither the monk nor Germano standing nearby could grab Diana's arm and hold her back. Ascanio threw his arms around the foolish woman, another young man took her by the feet. She resisted hardly at all and was carried out, lifted into her litter, and taken home.

Diana and Antiope were still facing one another, each paler than the other, Diana rueful and contrite after her rapidly exhausted fit of temper, Antiope struggling for words; she could as yet only stammer, she moved her lips noiselessly.

If the monk now grasped Antiope's hand in order to provide an escort to her who was mistreated by his betrothed, he was only fulfilling his chivalrous duty and his duty as host. Everyone found it natural. Especially Diana had to wish that the victim of her act of violence should disappear from her sight. She, too, then left with her father and brother. As for the gathered guests, they considered the most delicate thing to likewise disappear unto the last trace.

Bells rang under the sideboard table set out with amarellas   and Cyprian wine. A fool's cap appeared, and Gocciola crawled on all fours out of his delicious hiding place. Everything went off delightfully in his opinion; for he now had complete freedom to nibble on amarellas and empty one glass after another. In such manner he enjoyed himself for a while, until he heard steps approaching. He wanted to slip away, but giving a morose glance at the intruder, he judged any flight unnecessary. It was the monk who returned, and the monk was just as gleeful and intoxicated as he was; for the monk –

"Loved Antiope." The governor's lady friend interrupted the storyteller with a forced laugh.

"You have it, mistress, he loved Antiope," repeated Dante in a tragical tone.

"Naturally!" "How else?" "It had to be so!" "That's how it usually goes!" echoed back to the storyteller from all the circle of listeners.

"Careful, younglings," murmured Dante. "No, that's not how it usually goes. Is it then your opinion that a love with complete devotion of one's life and soul is an everyday occurrence, and do you even believe that you love or have been loved in that way? Undeceive yourselves! Everyone talks of ghosts, but few have seen them. I will give you an unobjectionable proof. There is knocking about this house a fashionable book of fables. Paging through it with careful fingers, I found among a lot of rubbish a true word. 'Love,' it says in one place, 'is rare and mostly comes to a bad end.'" Dante said this seriously. Then he was mocking: "Since you are all so fully learned and experienced in love and moreover since it does not become me to have a young man overpowered by passion speak through my toothless mouth, I will skip over the revealing soliloquy of the returning Astorre and say in brief: inasmuch as the prudent Ascanio overheard him, he became dismayed and preached reason to him."

"Will you mutilate your moving story so deplorably, my Dante?" The impetuous lady friend of the governor addressed herself with pleading hands to the Florentine. "Let the monk speak, so that we may experience how he turned away from a rough to a tender, from a cold to a feeling, from a stony to a beating heart –"

"Yes, Florentine," interrupted the governor's wife deeply moved and with darkly glowing cheeks, "let your monk speak, so that we can be amazed how it could happen that Astorre, as inexperienced and gullible as he was, betrayed a noble woman for a crafty one – haven't you noticed, Dante, that Antiope is a crafty woman? Little do you know women! In truth I tell you" – she raised her powerful arm and made a fist – "I too would have struck, not the poor foolish woman, but deliberately that guileful woman who at any cost wanted to bring herself to the attention of the monk." And she punched the air. The other woman flinched slightly.

Cangrande, who sat across from the two women and never stopped observing them, admired his wife and was delighted at her great passion. At this moment he found her incomparably lovelier than the more petite and delicate rival which he had given her, for the highest and deepest feelings achieve their expression only in a strong body and in a strong soul.

Dante, for his part, smiled for the first and only time on this evening, seeing that he had both women swaying so vigorously on the swing of his tale. He even went so far as to tease. "Ladies," he said. "What do you want from me? Talking to oneself is crazy. Did ever a wise man talk to himself?"

Now there arose out of the shadows a mischievous curly head, and a lad of the nobility, who must have been crouching in a cozy hiding spot behind some chair or the train of a lady's dress, called out heartily, "Great master, how little you know or pretend to know yourself! Know, Dante, no one chatters to himself more volubly than you, to such a degree that you ignore not only us dumb boys, but you even let Beauty pass close by you without greeting it."

"Really?" said Dante. "Where was that? where and when?"

"Well, yesterday on the Etsch bridge." The lad smiled. "You were leaning against the balustrade. The fetching Lucretia Nani went past, brushing against your toga. We boys were following, admiring her, and from the opposite direction strode two high-spirited soldiers, angling for a glance from her soft eyes. She, however, was seeking yours: for not everyone has strolled around hell unscathed! You, master, were looking at a rolling wave which was flowing down the middle of the Etsch river, and were mumbling something."

"I was sending a greeting to the sea. The wave was lovelier than the girl. But back to the two crazies! Listen, they are conversing! And, by the muses, from now on let no one interrupt me again, else midnight will find us still around the story-hearth."

As the monk, after he took Antiope home, again entered his hall – but I forgot to say that he did not meet Ascanio even though the latter took the same way with the litter and Madonna Olympia in it. For the nephew, after he had delivered the thoroughly demolished woman to her servants, had hurried immediately to his uncle, the tyrant, to serve up the wild proceedings to him as a fresh pastry. He preferred to inform Ezzelino of a city scandal than of a conspiracy.

I don't know whether the monk was as well-formed as the mocker Ascanio had made him out to be. But I see him, he who strides like the freshest blossoming youth. With winged feet he sweeps through the hall as if Zephyr carried him or Iris led him. His eyes are full of sunshine, and he murmurs sounds from the language of the blissful. Gocciola, who had drunk much Cyprian wine, likewise felt himself inspirited and rejuvenated. Under his soles as well the marble floor dissolved into white clouds. He felt an unquenchable thirst, like one bending over a spring, to listen in on the murmuring from the fresh lips of Astorre, and he began to measure the length of the hall next to the latter, now with stilted, now with skipping steps, with his fool's scepter under his arm.

"That tender head which offered itself for its father, also offered and gave itself for its mother!" whispered Astorre. "The modest head! how it burned! The mistreated head! how it suffered! The battered head! how it cried out! Has it ever left me since it lay on the block? It lived in my spirit. It accompanied me everywhere, it floated in my prayers, it shone in my cell, lay down on my pillow! Did not that lovely head with the white, slender neck lie next to that of St. Paul – "

"St. Paul?" sniggered the Droplet.

"St. Paul on our altarpiece – "

"With the curly black hair and the ruddy neck on the broad block and the axe of the executioner over it?" Gocciola occasionally said his prayers at the Franciscans.

The monk nodded. "I watched, then the axe flashed and I crumpled up in fear. Didn't I confess it to the prior?"

"And what did the prior say?" inquired Gocciola.

"My son," he said, "what you saw was a child of the heavenly triumphal procession who had rushed out ahead of the others. Fear nothing! No harm shall come to that ambrosial neck!"

"But," teased the wicked fool, "the child has grown so tall!" He raised his hand. Then he lowered it and held it just above the floor. "And the cowl of your Excellency," he smirked, "lies so low!"

This meanness could not affect the monk. A creative fire had travelled from Antiope's hand into his and began at first softly and delicately, then hotter and sharper, to burn in his veins. "Praise God the Father," he suddenly exulted, "who created man and woman!"

"Eve?" asked the fool.

"Antiope!" answered the monk.

"And the other one? The tall one? What are you going to do with her? Are your going to send her begging?" Gocciola wiped his eyes.

"What other one?" asked the monk. "Is there a woman who is not Antiope?"

That was too much even for the fool. He stared at Astorre appalled, but a fist grabbed him by the collar, dragged him to the portal and threw him into the hallway. The same hand then was laid on Astorre's shoulder.

"Awaken, sleepwalker!" cried the returning Ascanio, who had caught the last infatuated speech of the monk. He drew the entranced monk to a window seat, looked directly in the monk's eyes and: "Astorre, you are out of your mind!" he said to him.

The latter at first avoided the searching gaze as if blinded by it, then met it with his own, which was so full of jubilation as to depress Ascanio's gaze into timidity. "Are you surprised?" he said then.

"As little as at the blazing of a flame," returned Ascanio. "But since you are not a blind element but rather a reason and a will, stamp out the flame or else it will consume you and all of Padua. Must a worldling teach you divine and human law? You are married! So says this ring on your finger. If you now break your troth, as you did your monk's vows, you injure custom, duty, honor and the peace of the city. If you do not quickly and heroically draw the bolt of the blind god out of your heart, it will kill you, Antiope and yet a couple of others, whom it will just happen to hit.   Astorre! Astorre!

Ascanio's puckish lips were astonished at the august and serious words which in his trepidation he gave them to speak. "Your name," he said then, half jokingly, "is blaring like a trump and is calling you to struggle against yourself!"

Astorre plucked up his courage. "Someone has given me a love potion!" he cried. "I am raving, I am a crazy man! Ascanio, I give you authority over me. Shackle me!"

"I will shackle you to Diana!" said Ascanio. "Follow me, we will seek her!"

"Was it not Diana who struck Antiope?" asked the monk.

"That you dreamed! You dreamed everything! You were not in control of yourself! Come! I adjure you! I command you! I shall grab you and lead you!"

If Ascanio wanted to chase reality away, the steps of Germano ringing in the corridor brought it back. With a resolute face the brother of Diana came before the monk and grasped his hand. "A spoiled celebration, brother," he said. "My sister sent me – I lie, she didn't send me. She shut herself in her room, and inside she howls and curses her temper – today we are drowning in female tears! She loves you, only she cannot bring herself to say it. In runs in the family: I can't do it either. She did not doubt you for an instant. It is simple: you got rid of a ring somewhere – if it was your ring that the little Canossa – what's her name? right: Antiope! – was wearing. Her crazy mother found it and spun her fairy tale from it. Antiope is naturally innocent of all that as a newborn babe – anyone who thinks differently will have me to deal with!"

"Not I!" cried Astorre. "Antiope is as pure as heaven! The ring rolled away by accident!" and he told the story in hasty words.

"But also, Astorre, you can't hold it against my sister who attacked," asserted Germano. "The blood went to her head, she did not see who was in front of her. She thought to strike the crazy woman who was abusing her parents, and hit the dear innocent. She, however, must be restored to honor and dignity before God and man. Let me take care of that, brother-in-law! I am her brother. It will be simple."

"You talk on and on, but your meaning is obscure, Germano! What do you have in mind? How are you going to make it up to the poor thing?" asked Ascanio.

"It is simple," repeated Germano.   "I shall offer Antiope Canossa my hand and make her my wife!"

Ascanio put his hand to his forehead.   The idea stunned him.   But as he then, quickly reflecting, looked into the matter more closely, he found the heroic measure not so bad at all; but he threw an anxious glance at the monk.   The latter, again master of himself, kept quiet as a mouse and listened attentively.   The sense of honor of the warrior echoed through the wilderness of his soul like a clarion call.

"Thus I'll kill two birds with one stone, brother-in-law," explained Germano. "The maid will be established in her proper rank and honor.   I'd like to meet the man who would go whispering about my wife!   Too, I'll bring about peace between you as a married couple.   Diana won't have to be ashamed in your presence nor in her own and she is thoroughly cured of her rash temper.   I tell you: she is recovered from that her life long."

Astorre took his hand.   "You are good!" he said.   The will to overmaster his heavenly or earthly desire strengthened in the monk.   But this will was not free and this virtue not selfless; for it clung to a dangerous sophistry: just as I will embrace one I do not love, so too Antiope will be embraced by a man whom she will shortly marry in order to rectify an extraneous injustice. We all practice renunciation!   Self-denial and mortification in the world as in the monastery!

"What must happen, I will not put off," urged Germano. "Otherwise, she will toss and turn a sleepless night." I do not know if he meant Diana or Antiope. "Brother-in-law, you accompany me as witness: I will do it in proper form."

"No, no!" cried Ascanio dismayed. "Not Astorre! Take me!"

Germano shook his head. "Ascanio, my friend," he said, "you are not the right person for that. You are not a serious witness in matrimonial matters. And too, my brother Astorre would not let it be taken from him, to woo for me. It is indeed for the greatest part his own concern. Right, Astorre?" The latter nodded. "So get ready, brother-in-law. Make yourself presentable! Put on a gold chain!"

"And," Ascanio forced a joke, "when you cross the court, dip your head in the fountain. You yourself, however, Germano, are going to wear armor? So warlike? Is that appropriate for courting?"

"It is a long time since I have been out of armor, and it suits me. Why are you looking me over from head to foot, Asciano?"

"I am wondering where this armored man gets his certainty that he will not be thrown into the moat together with his scaling ladder?"

"That cannot be in question," said Germano calmly. "Will a girl who has been shamed and beaten turn down a knight? Then she'd be an even bigger fool than her mother.   That is but clear as day, Ascanio.   Come, Astorre."

While he who remained behind with his arms crossed thought over this new turn of events, whether it would lead to a playground of blossoming children or to a Camposanto[4], the youthful friends strode the short distance to the Canossa palace.

The cloudless day was fading into an evening of pure glowing gold, and listen! they are ringing the *Ave*. The monk said to himself his usual prayer, and his monastery, set somewhat above them, happened to extend by a pair of peacefully wistful strokes the familiar tones, with which the other bells of the town no longer competed. The monk too, felt blessed by the general peacefulness.

His glance fell on the face of his friend and dwelt on the weather-beaten features. They were radiant and joyful, made so without doubt by fulfilled duty, but also by the unconscious or unguarded happiness of reaching the port of a blessed island under the sail, filled with the wind of honor, of a chivalrous deed. "The sweet innocent," sighed the warrior.

With fierce rapidity the monk comprehended that the brother of Diana deceived himself if he considered himself selflessly disinterested, that Germano began to love Antiope, and was his rival. His breast felt a sharp

---

[4]   A famous burial ground in Pisa. [Translator's footnote]

sting, then a second even sharper one, such that he must have cried out. And now a whole nest of furious serpents swarmed and writhed in his bosom. Ladies and gentlemen, may God protect us all, men and women, from jealousy. It is the most excruciating agony, and who suffers from it, is more unfortunate than my damned!

With a grim visage and a constricted heart the monk followed the confident suitor up the steps of the palace at which they had arrived. It stood empty and desolate. Madonna Olympia must have locked herself in. No servants, and all the doors open. They passed through a row of already darkening chambers; at the threshold of the last chamber they stopped, for the young Antiope sat at the window.

Its arch, ending in the shape of a clover leaf, was full of the evening sunset which enveloped the charming figure in a half circle from bosom to neck. Her tousled crown of hair resembled the tips of a wreath of thorns, and the sighing lips sipped the heavens. The stricken young woman lay weary under the strain of the disgrace she had suffered, with closed eyes and limp arms; but in the quiet of her heart she rejoiced over and prized her disgrace, for this had united her for ever with Astorre.

And is not even today and until the end of days the highest love kindled by the deepest pity? Who can withstand the sight of the lovely when it suffers unjustly? I am not blaspheming, and I understand the difference, but even the Divine was beaten, and we kiss his welts and wounds.

Antiope did not wonder whether Astorre loved her. She knew it. There was no doubt. She was more convinced of that than of her breathing or the beating of her heart. She had not exchanged a syllable with Astorre from the first step of the path that they trod together. Their hands did not hold each other more firmly at the last: they grew together without gripping one another. They permeated each other, like two airy spiritual flames and, still upon parting were hardly to be loosed from each other, like roots from the earth.

Antiope laid hands on another's property and committed robbery against Diana almost in innocence, for she had neither a conscience any longer nor even any self-awareness. Padua, which lay before her with its towers, her mother, the monk's engagement, Diana, the entire earth, everything was annihilated: everything but the abyss of heaven, and that filled with light and love.

Astorre had wrestled with himself from the first step of the stairs to the last, and believed he had eked out a victory. I will achieve the sacrifice, he boasted to himself, and stand by the side of Germano as he woos her. On the top step he called on all his saints, most of all St. Francis, the master of self-command. He took hold of his heart, and believed that, through their spiritual assistance, he, as strong as Hercules, had strangled the serpents.   But the saint with the four stigmata had turned away from the disloyal disciple, who had rejected his cincture and habit.

Meanwhile, Germano, standing next to him, composed his speech, but was unable to get further than the two arguments which had occurred to him at the very first. Besides, he was in good spirits – he had given speeches to his soldiers many times in campaigns – and he was not afraid of a girl. But he could endure the waiting just as little as before a battle. He clinked his sword lightly against his armor.

Antiope took affright, looked up, quickly got up and stood, her back to the window and facing, with a darkening countenance, the men who were bowing to her in the twilight.

"Be at ease, Antiope Canossa!" spoke Germano, "I bring this man, Astorre Vicedomini, whom people call the monk, the husband of my sister Diana, with me as a valid witness: see, I have come to seek your hand from you yourself, since you have no father and such a mother. My sister forgot herself with you" – he struggled against using a stronger word and thereby betraying Diana, whom he adored – "and I, her brother, have come to make amends for the bad that my sister did. Diana and Astorre, you and I, each coming part way toward the other, you women will take each other's hands."

This rude comparison of the abuser and the suffering one, the striker and the struck, wounded the sensitive mind of the monk listening to it – or was an adder stirring? "Germano, that's not how one woos!" he murmured to the armored one.

The latter heard it, and since the dark Antiope remained as quiet as a mouse, he became upset. He felt that he should speak more softly, and he spoke more gruffly. "Without a father and with such a mother," he repeated, "you have need of a man's protection! You were able to find that out today, young lady. You won't want to be humiliated and beaten in front of all Padua a second time! Give yourself to me, as you are, and I will protect you from the top of your head to your feet!" Germano thought of his armor.

Astorre found this courting of appalling harshness: Germano, as it appeared to him, dealt with Antiope as a prisoner of war – or was a serpent hissing? – "That's not how one woos, Germano!" he whispered. The latter half turned, "If you know how to do it better, then you woo for me, brother-in-law," he said sullenly. He stepped aside to give him room.

Then Astorre approached her, got down on one knee, raised his hands with steepled fingertips, and his anxious glances questioned the delicate head against the pale golden background. "Does love find words?" he stammered. Twilight and silence.

Finally Antiope whispered: "For whom are you asking, Astorre?"

"For this man here, my brother, Germano."   He forced it out.   Then she hid her countenance in her hands.

Now did Germano lose his patience.   "I'll speak plainly to you," he burst out, and: "short and to the point, Antiope Canossa," he roughly grabbed the girl, "will you be my wife or not?"

Antiope shook her head slowly and gently, but in spite of the growing darkness with a clear negation.

"I have my refusal," said Germano tonelessly. "Come, brother!" and he quitted the room with steps just as firm as had used on entering.   But the monk did not follow him.

Astorre remained in his supplicating position.   Then, trembling himself, he took Antiope's trembling hands and removed them from her countenance.   Which mouth sought the other, I do not know, for the room had become completely dark.

Also it became so quiet that, were their ears not full of tempestuous exultation and blissful choirs, they could have easily heard mumbled prayers in an adjoining chamber.   It came about thus: next to Antiope's room, down a few steps, was the palace chapel, and the morrow was the third anniversary of the death of Count Canossa.   After midnight the requiem mass was to be read in the presence of the widow and the orphan.   The priests had already installed themselves, awaiting the acolytes.

No more than the subterranean mumbling did the pair hear the shuffling slippers of the Madonna Olympia, who was looking for her daughter and now, in the thin light of the candlestick which she held in her hand, quietly and attentively observed the lovers. That the most audacious lie of an extravagant imagination became truth and fact before her eyes in these tenderly embracing figures, about that madonna Olympia did not marvel; but let it be said to the crazy woman's credit, just as little did she taste the pleasure of vengeance. She did not gloat over the bitter suffering in store for the violent Diana, rather the simple maternal joy prevailed of seeing her child valued at her worth, desired and loved.

Since now, having been struck by a sharp ray from her light, the two looked up startled, she asked in a soft and natural voice, "Astorre Vicedomini, do you love Antiope Canossa?"

"More than anything, Madonna," answered the monk.

"And you will defend her?"

"Against the world!" cried Astorre boldly.

"So is it right." She affirmed him. "But, you mean it truly, right? You will never cast her away, like Diana? You are not trying to make a fool of me? You won't make a poor crazy woman, as they call me, unhappy?

You won't let my child be disgraced again? You are not going to look for any evasions or delays? You will give my eyes assurance, and lead Antiope to the altar right away, like a devout Christian and valiant nobleman? And you do not have far to go for a priest. Do you hear that murmuring? There's one on his knees down there."

And she opened a low door behind which a pair of steep steps led down into the palace sanctuary. Astorre looked down: below the crude arch a barefooted man prayed before a small altar in the uncertain light of a candle. The man was not dissimilar to him in age and figure, and also he wore the habit and cincture of St. Francis.

I believe that this barefooted man must have been on his knees praying here and at just this time by divine providence to warn and to frighten Astorre for the last time. But in his flaming arteries the medicine became poison. As he beheld the embodiment of his monastic life, a defiant spirit of daring and certitude came over him. With these same feet I got around my first vow, he laughed, and look, the barrier fell under my leap – why not the second also? My saints have allowed me to succumb! Perhaps they will save and protect the sinner! The frenzied man seized Antiope and dragged her, rather than led her, down the stairs; madonna Olympia, however, who after a brief moment of lucidity, again lost her wits, slammed the door closed behind the monk and her child, as if behind a successful catch, a snared prey, and eavesdropped through the keyhole.

What she saw remains uncertain. According to the opinion of the common people, Astorre threatened the barefooted man with drawn sword and forced him. That is impossible, for the man Astorre had never in his life worn a sword. It may be closer to the truth that the barefooted man – sad to say – was a bad monk and perhaps the same purse found its way under his habit that Astorre had taken when he went to buy the wedding band for Diana.

That however, at first the priest balked, that the two monks argued with one another, that the ponderous arches hid an ugly scene – such I read in the distorted and horrified face of the eavesdropper. Donna Olympia understood that there below a sacrilege was being committed, and as the instigator and accessory thereto she subjected herself to the severity of the law and the vengeance of the betrayed parties, and since it was the anniversary of the execution of the count, her husband, she believed her head too, irretrievably forfeited to the ax. She imagined she heard the approaching step of Ezzelino: whereupon she fled and cried, "Help! Murder!"

The tortured woman rushed into the hallway and to the window which looked out into the inner court. "My mule! My litter!" she cried to those below, and the servants of the crazy woman, laughing at the double command – the mule was for the country, the litter for the town – got up slowly and lazily out of a corner, where they were drinking and playing dice by the light of a lantern made from a gourd. An old equerry, who alone remained faithful to the unfortunate mistress, worriedly saddled two mules and led them through the gateway into the forecourt of the palace which adjoined the lane: he had accompanied Donna Olympia on a number of fool's errands before. The others, cracking jokes, followed with the litter.

On the great steps the fleeing crazy woman, who had forgotten her beloved child in the overpowering drive for self-preservation which arose from the disaster, ran into Ascanio, who was concerned, having been left without any news, and driven by disquiet, had gone out to seek information.

"What has happened, Signora?" he asked hurriedly.

"A disaster," she croaked, like a raven taking wing, ran down the steps, sat on her animal, dug her furious heels into it, and disappeared into the darkness.

Ascanio looked through the darkened rooms until he came to the chamber of Antiope, lit by the light which Madonna Olympia had left there. As he looked around, the door to the palace chapel was opened, and two lovely specters came up from the depths. The valiant Ascanio began to tremble. "Astorre, you are married to her!" The resonant name boomed in the echo of the vaulted ceilings like a trump of those days. "And you are wearing Diana's ring on your finger!"

Astorre tore it off and flung it away.

Ascanio shot to the open window through which the ring had flown. "It slid into a crack between two paving stones," said a voice from the street. Ascanio saw turbans and helmets. It was the governor's people, who were beginning their nightly rounds.

"A word with you, Abu Mohammed!" Quickly gathering his wits, he called to an old man with a white beard, who politely replied, "Your wish is my command!" and with two other Saracens and a German disappeared into the gate of the palace.

Abu-Mohammed-al-Tabib guarded not only the safety of the streets, but also entered the innermost parts of the houses in order to arrest traitors to the Empire – or what the Governor called traitors to the Empire. Emperor Frederick had given him to his son-in-law, the tyrant, so that he would recruit for the latter a Saracenic body guard, and he remained in Padua at the head of it. Abu Mohammed was quite a phenomenon and had winning ways. He sympathized with the distress of the family whose member he led to the dungeon or to the block, and comforted the afflicted in his broken Italian with sayings of Arabian poets. I suspect that even if he did possess certain surgical knowledge and concepts, he had first and foremost to thank for his sobriquet "al Tabib," that is, the physician, certain physician-like manners: encouraging hand gestures, calming words, as for example, "This won't hurt," or, "It will pass," with which the followers of Galen used to introduce a painful operation. In short, Abu Mohammed handled the tragic gently and was at the time of my tale, in spite of his strict and bitter office, not a detested personality in Padua. Later, when the tyrant found it enjoyable to torture human bodies – which you will not be able to believe, Cangrande! – Abu Mohammed left him and returned to his gracious Emperor.

At the threshold of the chamber, Abu Mohammed motioned to his three attendants to remain. The German, who was carrying the torch, a truculent looking fellow, did not remain long. He had accompanied Germano this day to vespers at the Vicedomini palace and the latter told him laughingly: "Leave me now! I am going to betroth my little sister to the monk!" The German knew the sister of his commander, and had a kind of quiet affection towards her, on account of her great height and her honest eyes. Since he now saw the monk, at whose side he had ridden that day at noon, hand in hand with a small, delicate female, who appeared to him, next to the large image of Diana, as a doll, he smelled a betrayal, angrily threw the torch to the floor, whence one of the Saracens carefully picked it up, and hurried away to inform Germano of the monk's perfidiousness.

Ascanio, who guessed the German's purpose, asked Abu Mohammed to call him back. The latter however refused. "He would not obey," he said softly, "and would beat down two or three of my men. Of what other service, Sir, may I be to you? Should I arrest these blossoming youth?"

"Astorre, they want to separate us!" cried Antiope, and sought protection in the arms of the monk. The girl who had committed sacrilege at the altar had lost her natural fearlessness together with her innocence. The monk, whose guilt rather emboldened and inspired him, took a step toward the Saracen and suddenly snatched his sword from its scabbard. "Careful, lad, you might cut yourself," warned the latter good-naturedly.

"Let me tell you, Abu Mohammed, " explained Ascanio, "this impassioned man is the playmate of my youth and was for a long time the monk Astorre, whom you have surely seen on the streets of Padua. His own father duped him out of his monastic vows and engaged him to an unloved woman. A few hours ago he exchanged rings with her, and now, as you see him here, he is the husband of this other one."

"Fate!"   The Saracene rendered his judgment placidly.

"And the one betrayed," continued Ascanio, "is Diana Pizzaguerra, the sister of Germano! You know him. He believes and trusts for a long time, but let him see and understand that he has been cheated and deceived, then the blood shoots to his head and he kills."

"No doubt about it," confirmed Abu Mohammed. "He is German on his mother's side, and they are children of loyalty."

"Advise me, Saracen. I know of only one way out: perhaps a salvation. We bring the matter before the governor. Ezzelino might set things right. In the meantime, let your people guard the monk in his own solid house. I will hurry to my uncle. But you take this young woman, Abu Mohammed, to the margravine Cunizza, the sister of the governor, the pious and genial Domina, who has been holding court here for several weeks. Take the pretty sinner. I entrust her to your white beard." "That you may," assured Mohammed.

Antiope clung to the monk and cried out even more piteously than the first time: "They want to separate me from you! Don't leave me, Astorre! Not for an hour! Not for a moment! Or I'll die!" The monk raised his sword.

Ascanio, who detested all violence, looked questioningly at the Saracen. The latter regarded with paternal eyes the two who were holding on to each other. "Let the shadows embrace!" he then said in a soft voice, whether because he was a philosopher and considered life as mere appearance, or whether because he wanted to say: perhaps Ezzelino will sentence them to death tomorrow, so do not begrudge the love struck butterflies their hour!

Ascanio did not doubt the reality of things; so much the more was he amenable to the second sense of the utterance. Not only as the happy-go-lucky fellow that he was, but also as a kind-hearted and humane person, he hesitated to tear the lovers apart.

"Astorre," he asked, "do you know me?"

"You were my friend," answered the latter.

"And still am. You have none more faithful."

"Oh, do not separate me from her!" The monk now begged in such an affecting tone that Ascanio did not resist. "So stay together," he said, "until you appear before the court." He whispered with Abu Mohammed.

The latter approached the monk, gently relieved him of the sword, loosening finger by finger his grip, and let it fall back into the scabbard on his hip. Then he went to the window, motioned to his company, and the Saracens took possession of the litter of Madonna Olympia which had been left in the forecourt.

Through a narrow, dark lane the rapid flight proceeded: Antiope in front, carried by four Saracens, to her side the monk and Ascanio, then the turbans. Abu Mohammed concluded the procession.

The latter hurried to a small plaza and across from a lighted church. Segueing into the dark continuation of the lane, he roughly collided with another procession coming the other way, which procession was accompanied by a great many people.   Fierce squabbling arose. "Make way for La Sposina!" cried the crowd.   Choir boys brought long candles from the church and shielded their fluttering flames with their hands. The yellow glow showed a slanting litter and an overturned stretcher. La Sposina was a bride from among the people who had died and was being taken to be buried. She did not stir and let herself quietly be laid back on her stretcher. But the gathered common folk saw the monk, who held Antiope in a protective embrace, and they knew, however, that the monk that day had married Diana Pizzaguerra. Abu Mohammed established order.   Without further incident they reached the palace.

Astorre and Antiope were received by the servants with astonished and dismayed glances.   They disappeared into the gate without having taken leave of Abu Mohammed and Ascanio. The latter wrapped himself tightly in his cloak and accompanied for a few steps the Saracen, who went around the municipal palace which it was his duty to guard, counting the gates and, looking up, measuring its walls.

"An eventful day," said Ascanio.

"A blessed night," replied the Saracen, looking at the heavens bestrewn with stars. The eternal lights, whether or not they govern our destinies, wandered according to their placid laws until a new day, the newest and last of Astorre and Antiope, brandished the divine torch.

In the morning of that same day the tyrant was listening with his nephew through a small arched window of his city tower to the small adjoining plaza which an excited crowd occupied, murmuring and roaring like the changing billows of the sea.

The encounter of the day before of the litter with the stretcher and the tumult arising therefrom had become known through the whole town as quick as lightening. All heads busied themselves, waking or dreaming, with nothing else than the monk and his wedding: not only his vows to heaven was the blasphemous man supposed to have broken, but also now to the earth, he was said to have betrayed his bride, thrown away his ring, in frenzied rapid reversal of a suddenly inflamed mind taken a new wife, a fifteen-year old, the blossom of life, and out of the ruptured monk's habit a greedy bird of prey was supposed to have taken wing. But the just tyrant, who was said to be no respecter of persons, was supposed to have had the house which sheltered the two criminals guarded by his Saracens; it was said that today he would, soon, now bring the misdeed of the two gentlefolk – for the young sinner was said to be a Canossa – before his judgment seat, give justice to the chaste Diana, and throw the bloody heads of the two guilty ones out of the window to the virtuous common folk, who were offended by the bad example of his nobles.

The tyrant, while he kept an observing eye on the seething crowd, had Ascanio report to him the events of the day before. The falling in love did not affect him; only the ring having rolled to Antiope engaged him for a moment as a new form of fate. "I find fault," he said, "with your not tearing them apart yesterday! I commend your guarding them! The marriage to Diana retains its validity. The sacrament which was extorted by the sword or bought with a purse is as nugatory as possible. The priest who let himself be frightened or bribed deserves the gallows, and if he is caught, then he will swing. Again, why didn't you step between the irresponsible one and the child? why didn't you rip the bewildered girl out of the arms of the intoxicated man? You gave her to him! Now they are man and wife."

Ascanio, who had ·recovered his brightness and flippancy through sleep, repressed a smile. "Epicure!" Ezzelino rebuked him. But he flattered his uncle: "It is done, stern uncle. If you bring the case under your authority, everything is rescued. I have arranged for both parties to appear humbly before your judgment seat at nine o'clock this morning." A bell tower across the way struck the hour. "If only you will, your firm and wise hand can cut the knot easily. Love is profligate, and greed knows nothing of honor. The lovestruck monk will give to that contemptible miser, which we all know the worthy Pizzaguerra to be, whatever he demands. Of course Germano will draw his sword, but you order him to re-sheath it. He is your man. He will grit his teeth, but he will obey."

"I wonder," said Ezzelino, "if I do right in withdrawing the monk from the sword of my Germano. Should Astorre live? Can he, now – after the discarded sandal, he has trodden the assumed gentlemanly shoe into a floppy slipper and has distorted the *cantus firmus*[5] of the monk into a clangorous street ditty? I – for my part – will do what I can to preserve the existence of the fickle and worthless man. Only, I can do nothing against his fate. If Astorre is destined for Germano's sword, then I can order the latter to put it down, but the former would run into it. I know that. I have experienced it." And he fell into brooding.

Timidly Ascanio directed his gaze sideways. He knew a terrible history.

Once the tyrant had captured a castle, and he ordered the rebels who held it put to the sword. The first available soldier wielded the sword. There knelt, to received the death stroke, a handsome youth whose features mesmerized Ezzelino. Ezzelino thought he recognized his own and asked the youth about his origins. He was the son of a woman whom Ezzelino in his youth had loved sinfully. He pardoned the

---

5   The traditional unisonal plainchant of the Church.
[Translator's footnote]

condemned youth. The youth, haunted by his own curiosity and goaded by the jealous teasing of those who had lost their sons or relations to that bloody order, did not rest until he had unraveled the mystery of his preference. He was supposed to have brandished a dagger against his own mother and forced the evil secret from her. The revelation of his illegitimate birth poisoned his young soul. He conspired anew against the tyrant, attacked him in the street, and was struck down by the same soldier, who fortuitously was the first one to rush to Ezzelino's aid, with the selfsame sword.

Ezzelino buried his head in his right arm for a time and contemplated the demise of his son. Then he slowly raised it and asked, "But what will become of Diana?"

Ascanio shrugged his shoulders. "Diana is star-crossed. She has lost two men, the one in the Brenta, the other to a lovelier woman. And on top of that the stingy father! She will enter a nunnery. What else is there for her?"

Now from the plaza below arose a grumbling, a complaining, a cursing, a menacing. "Murder the monk!" goaded individual voices, but just as they were about to unite themselves in a general cry, the people's anger transformed in a strange manner into an astonished and wondering "Ah!" "Ah, how lovely she is!" The tyrant and Ascanio were able comfortably to observe the scene: Saracens on slender berber horses encircling the monk Astorre and his young wife, who were carried on mules. The new Vicedomini rode with her veil down. But as the thousand fists of the people were raised at the monk, her husband, she passionately threw herself in front of him. This loving gesture tore her veil. It was not the attractiveness of her face alone, nor the youthfulness of her form, but rather the complete play of her soul, the acted-out feeling, the breath of her life, which disarmed and enraptured the crowd, just as it had the monk yesterday, who now rode in as a conquering hero with his freshly-captured prize, without the least trepidation, for he believed himself invincible and invulnerable.

Ezzelino regarded this triumph of beauty somewhat scornfully. He turned his eye eagerly towards the appearance of a second party, which was entering from another lane into the plaza in front of the tower. Three nobles, like Astorre and Antiope accompanied by many attendants, were seeking a path through the crowd. In the middle, a snow-white head: the worthy appearance of the old Pizzaguerra. To his left, Germano. He had raged dreadfully the day before, when the German had brought him news of the betrayal, and jumped straightway to vengeance, but was overtaken by the Saracen, who charged him, his father and his sister, to appear the next morning before the court of the governor at the tower. Thereupon he had disclosed the outrage of the monk to his sister, which he would have preferred to have kept from her until after having taken revenge, and had marveled at her composure. Diana rode to the right of her father, no differently than usual, except that she carried her broad neck a bit lower than yesterday as if due to the weight of a heavy thought.

The crowd, which a minute earlier would have greeted the injured woman and those seeking her vindication with enraged cheering, now, its eye still blinded by the radiance of Antiope and, comprehending the monk's betrayal and entering into his fault, was satisfied with murmuring a sympathetic, "Poor thing! Always a victim!"

Now the five appeared before the tyrant, who sat in an unfurnished hall on a chair raised up above the floor level by only two steps. Before him stood the complainants and the accused opposite each other: here, both Pizzaguerras and a little to the side, the large form of Diana; there, hand in hand, the monk and Antiope, all of them in awe, while Ascanio leaned against the high chair of the tyrant, as if he wanted to maintain his impartiality and the middle between the two companions of his youth.

"Gentlepeople," began Ezzelino, "I shall treat your case, not as a matter touching the state, where a breach of faith is betrayal, and betrayal is *lèse majesté*, but as a remediable family matter. Indeed, the Pizzaguerras, the Vicedominis, the Canossas are of just as noble blood as I, only that the majesty of the Emperor has made me your governor in your land." Ezzelino bowed his head upon mentioning the highest authority; he could not bare his head because, whenever he did not cover it with a battle helm, he wore no headcovering, according to the ancient manner, even in heavy wind and bad weather. "Thus the twelve houses form a large family, to which I also belong through my grandmother. But how we have dwindled by the disastrous blindness and culpable rebellion of some against the highest secular authority! If you believe me, then we shall save, insofar as we are able, what we still have. To this end I have held back the vengeance of the Pizzaguerras against Astorre Vicedomino, although I consider it in its nature just. If you," he turned to the three Pizzaguerras, "are not in agreement with my leniency, then hear and consider this: I, Ezzelino da Romano, am the first and the most guilty. If I had not let my horse run along the Brenta on a certain day at a certain hour, Diana would be properly married, and this one would be mumbling his breviary. Had I not ordered my Germans to muster on a certain day and at a certain hour, then my Germano would not have seated the monk on a horse at an inopportune time and the latter would have taken back from the woman whom he now holds by the hand, the wedding band which was rolled to her by his evil daemon – "

"By my good daemon!" The monk exulted.

" – which was rolled to her by his daemon. Therefore, gentlepeople, favor me by helping me unravel and resolve this complicated matter; for if you insisted on strictness, then I would have to also condemn myself and myself first!"

This unusual speech did not discompose the old Pizzaguerra in the least, and when the tyrant addressed him: "Noble sir, you are the complainant," he said short and crisp, "Excellency, Astorre Vicedomini publicly and in full accord with received custom betrothed himself to my child Diana. Then, however, without Diana having committed any offense against him, he broke his betrothal. Without cause, against the law, disgracing the Church. This action weighs heavily and demands, if not blood, which your Excellency does not want to see spilled, a heavy penalty," and he made the gesture of a shopkeeper, laying counterweight against counterweight in a scale.

"Without Diana having committed any offense?" repeated the tyrant. "It appears to me she committed an offense. Did she not have a crazy woman before her? And Diana reviled and smote. For Diana is hot-tempered and unreasonable if she believes she has been injured in her rights."

Here Diana nodded and said, "You speak the truth, Ezzelino."

"That's also why," continued the tyrant, "Astorre turned his heart away from her: he beheld a barbarian."

"No, lord," contradicted the monk, insulting the betrayed woman yet again, "I was not observing Diana, but rather that sweet countenance which received the blow, and I was moved to pity in my bowels."

The tyrant shrugged his shoulders. "You see, Pizzaguerra," he smiled, "the monk is like a prim maiden who has sipped strong wine for the first time, and then behaves accordingly. However, we are mature, sober people. Let us see how this matter can be dealt with."

Pizzaguerra responded, "Much, Ezzelino, would I do to please you on account of your services to Padua. But can injury to the honor of one's house be expiated other than by a naked sword?" Thus spake the father of Diana and he made with his arm a noble gesture, which however degenerated into a gesticulation which appeared similar to an opened up hand, if not a hand reaching for an exchange.

"Offer, Astorre!" said the governor, with the double meaning of: offer your hand, or offer money and property!

"Lord," the monk now turned to the tyrant forthrightly and nobly, "if you see in me one who is unstable, even senseless, I do not take it amiss, for a more powerful god, whom I disavowed because I could not sense his existence, has revenged himself on me and overpowered me. Even now he drives me like a storm and whirls my cloak over my head. If I have to pay for my happiness – beggarly word! paltry language! – if I have to pay for the highest in life with my life: I comprehend it and find the price set low! But if I may live and live with her, then I will not haggle." He smiled blissfully. "Take whatever I own, Pizzaguerra!"

"Gentlepeople," decreed the tyrant, "I shall act as guardian for this profligate youth. We will negotiate together, Pizzaguerra. You heard it: I have broad authority. What do you think of the Vicedomini mines, Pizzaguerra?"

The respectable old man was silent, but his close-set eyes glittered like two diamonds.

"Take my pearl fisheries too!" called out Astorre, but Ascanio, who came gliding down the steps, shut his mouth.

"Noble Pizzaguerra," Ezzelino made another attempt on the old man, "take the mines! I know that the honor of your house concerns you more than anything and is not for sale at any price, but I also know that you are a good Paduan and will do something for the sake of the peace of the town!"

The old man kept a stubborn silence.

"Take the vein," repeated Ezzelino, who loved to make a play on words, "and give the veil!"

"The mines and the fisheries?" asked the old man, as if he were hard of hearing.

"The mines, I said, and that's enough. They produce many thousands of pounds. If you were to demand more, Pizzaguerra, then I would be mistaken about your attitude, and you would make yourself subject to the ugly suspicion that you were putting honor up for sale."

Since the moneygrubber feared the tyrant and could not obtain any more, he swallowed his vexation and offered the monk his desiccated hand. "Put it in writing, as a permanent witness," he then said, and drew from his purse a stylus and account book, drafted the deed with trembling fingers "coram domino Azzolino" and had the monk sign it. Whereupon, he bowed to the governor and requested to be excused, despite being one of the twelve, from attending the wedding of the monk, on account of the debilities of age.

Germano had stood next to his father, suppressing his anger. Now he took off one of his iron gloves. He would have flung it in the face of the monk, had not a restraining gesture of the tyrant bidden him stop.

"Son, would you break the peace?" The old Pizzaguerra now also admonished him. "My word once given encompasses and guarantees yours as well. Obey! By my oath! By your inheritance!" he threatened.

Germano laughed. "You take care of your filthy dealings, father!' he spat out scornfully. But even you, Ezzelino, Lord of Padua, cannot deny me. It is a man's right and a personal matter. If I refuse obedience to the Emperor and you, his governor, then lop off my head; but you cannot stop me, fair-minded as you are, from strangling this monk, who has made a monkey of my sister and has deceived me. If infidelity were without consequence, who would want to live? There is not enough room on this earth for the monk and me. He himself will understand that when he returns to his senses."

"Germano," commanded Ezzelino, "I am your military commander. Perhaps tomorrow the trump will sound. You are not your own, you belong to the Empire!"

Germano did not respond. He affixed his glove. "A long time ago," he said then, "among the blind heathen there was a deity which avenged breaches of loyalty. That will not have changed with the ringing of church bells. To that deity I commend my cause!" Swiftly he raised his hand.

"It is good so," smiled Ezzelino. "This evening a masked wedding reception will be celebrated in the palace of the Vicedomini, exactly according to the usual custom. I shall be the host and I invite you, Germano and Diana. No armor, Germano! Wear a short sword!"

"Brute!" groaned the warrior. "Come, father! Why would you prolong the display of our disgrace?" He dragged the old man away with him.

"And you, Diana," asked Ezzelino, since he saw only her and the newlyweds still before his seat. "Are you not going with your father and brother?"

"If you will permit it, Lord," she said, "I have a word to speak to the new Vicedomini." Looking past the monk she fastened her glance on Antiope.

The latter, whose hand Astorre did not release, had taken a passive but deeply felt interest in the court of the tyrant.   In a trice the enamored woman blushed. Then the color drained from the face of a guilty woman as she discovered beneath the smile and the graciousness of Ezzelino his real judgment condemning her.   Then rejoiced a child who has evaded punishment. Then arose the first self-assurance of the young lady, the new Vicedomini.   Now, addressed directly by Diana, she gave her a shamefaced and hostile look.

The latter did not let herself be distracted.   "Look here, Antiope!" she said.   "Here, my finger," she stretched it forth, "wears the ring of your husband.   You dare not forget it.   I am not more superstitious than others, but in your place I would be uneasy.   You have committed a serious sin against me, but I will be gracious and lenient.   This evening you will celebrate the wedding with masks according to custom.   I will appear.   Come contrite and humbly and take the ring from my finger!"

Antiope uttered a cry of fear and clung to her husband.   Then, enveloped in his arms, she spoke vehemently, "I should abase myself?   What is your command, Astorre?   My honor is your honor.   I am nothing but your property, your heartbeat, your breath, and your soul. If you desire it, and command it, then!"

Astorre spoke to Diana, tenderly soothing his wife, "She will do it.   May her humility conciliate you! and mine too! Be my guest this evening and remain favorably disposed towards my house!" He turned to Ezzelino, thanked him respectfully for his judgment and his clemency, bowed, and took away his wife. But at the doorway he turned toward Diana questioningly, "And in which costume will you appear, so that we may recognize you and show honor towards you?"

The latter smiled contemptuously. Again she turned to Antiope. "I shall come as the one which I call myself and which I am: the untouched, the virginal!" she said proudly. Then she repeated, "Antiope, think about it: contrite and humble!"

"Do you mean it sincerely, Diana? You have nothing up your sleeve?" doubted the tyrant, as now the Pizzaguerra woman stood facing him alone.

"Nothing," she replied, disdaining any assurance.

"And what will become of you, Diana?" he asked.

"Ezzelino," she answered bitterly, "here before your judgment seat my father bartered away the honor and right of vengeance of his child for a couple of clods of dirt. I am not worthy that the sun should shine on me. For such is the nunnery!" And she left the hall.

"Most splendid uncle!" rejoiced Ascanio. "You are marrying the happiest couple in Padua and making out of a dangerous situation an exciting fairy tale with which I shall some day, as a venerable old man, delight my grandsons and granddaughters in front of the fireplace!"

"Idyllic nephew!" scoffed the tyrant. He went to the window and looked down on the plaza, where the crowd waited in feverish curiosity. Ezzelino had ordered that those to whom he had granted an audience be let out through a rear gateway.

"Paduans!" he declaimed in a loud voice, and thousands fell silent as a desert. "I have looked into the business. It was complicated, and there was fault on both sides. I forgave, for I am always inclined to clemency whenever the majesty of the Empire is not concerned. This evening Astorre Vicedomini and Antiope Canossa will hold a masked wedding celebration. I, Ezzelino, am the host of the fete, and I invite you all. Eat hearty, for the treat is on me! To you will belong the taverns and the streets. But let no one enter the Vicedomini palace nor menace me, otherwise, by my hand! – and now let everyone return quietly to his own business, if you have affection for me!"

An uncertain murmuring rose up. It subsided and faded away.

"How they love you!" joked Ascanio.

Dante paused for breath. Then he finished in rapid phrases.

After the tyrant had held court, he rode at midday to one of his forts which was under construction. He desired to return to Padua in time to observe Antiope's humbling herself before Diana.

However, contrary to expectation and against his will he was detained at the castle, which was several miles distant from the town. Thither a dust-covered Saracen came galloping to him and handed him a hand-written letter of the Emperor, which required immediate answer. The matter was of importance. Shortly before, Ezzelino had attacked by night and captured an imperial castle in Ferrara, in whose commander, a Sicilian, Ezzelino's sharp eye had suspected a traitor, and had put the ambivalent imperial castellan in chains. Now the Hohenstaufen demanded an accounting for this smart, but audacious, invasion of his dominion. Resting his furrowed brow in his left hand, Ezzelino made his right glide over the parchment, and his stylus drew him onward from the first to the second to a third. He discussed thoroughly with his illustrious father-in-law the possibilities and objectives of an impending, or at least planned, campaign. Thus the hours and his sense of time disappeared. Only when he had again mounted his horse did he recognize from the change in the stars, about which he was knowledgeable – they twinkled in utter clarity – that he would barely reach Padua by midnight. Leaving his retinue far behind him, as rapidly as a spirit he flew over the darkened plains. But he chose his path and carefully rode around a shallow ditch which the daring rider would have easily put behind him on another day: he forestalled fate from threatening his ride and downing his stallion. Once more, on his stretched courser he devoured the open space, but the lights of Padua would not appear.

There, in front of the wide city palace of the Vicedomini, while darkness grew upon it in the quickly increasing dusk, the drunken commoners had gathered. Licentious scenes alternated with comical ones in the not large plaza. In the close-packed crowd an angry passion was brewing, a bacchanalian frenzy, to which the youths dismissed from the upper school contributed an element of ridicule and joking.

Now a tedious cantilena became audible, in the nature of a litany, like our peasants used to sing. It was a procession of farmers, young and old, from one of the countless villages which belonged to the Vicedomini. These poor people, who in their remoteness had heard nothing about the monk's leaving his monastery, but only in vague outlines of the marriage of the heir, had started out before daybreak with the usual wedding gifts and now reached their destination after a lengthy pilgrimage in the dust of the country road. They stopped and gathered together, slowly moving forward across the surging plaza, here a curly-headed boy, almost still a child, with a golden honey comb, there, a shy, proud lass with a bleating, beribboned lamb in her caring arms. All sought eagerly after the countenance of their new lord.

Now they gradually disappeared in the arch of the gateway, where right and left the burning torches blazed in their iron rings, contending with the last light of the day. In the gateway, Ascanio was shouting orders, as the steward of the feast, he, who was otherwise so friendly, in an irritated voice.

From hour to hour a spirit of wantonness increased among the common people, and when the elegant masqueraders finally arrived, they were jostled, the servants had their torches torn out of their hands and stamped out on the stone pavement, the noble wives separated from their husbands and lewdly teased, unavenged by a sword stroke, which on a normal evening would have immediately punished such insolence.

To such an extent that not far from the palace gate a tall woman in the costume of a Diana was fighting with a ring of schoolboys and clergy of the lowest order closing in on her. A gaunt man showed off his knowledge of mythology. "You're not Diana," he said flirtatiously through his nose, "you are someone else! I recognize you. Here sits your turtle dove!" and he pointed to the silver half-moon above the goddess's forehead. The latter, however, did not flatter like Aphrodite, but rather fulminated like Artemis. "Get away, swine!" she rebuked him. "I am a pure goddess and detest the clergy!" "Cooo, cooo," mimicked the bean pole and groped with his bony hands, but at once let out a piercing cry. Whimpering, the wretch held up his hand and showed his injury. It was stuck quite through and spurted blood: the infuriated wench had reached behind her into her quiver – the misappropriated hunting quiver of her brother – and with a razor-sharp arrow chastised the loathsome hand.

This rapid performance was quickly supplanted by another just as horrible, if not as bloody. A musical procession, mixing together every conceivable contrariety and strident dissonance, and which resembled a raging altercation of the damned in hell, forged a path through the stunned and enthralled crowd. The lowest and worst class of persons – cutpurses, pimps, whores, beggars – blared, rasped, beat, whistled, squealed, bleated, and groaned in front of and behind a fantastical couple. A tall, brutalized woman of ruined beauty walked arm in arm with a drunken monk in a tattered habit. This was the monastic brother Serapion, who, spurred on by Astorre's example, escaped from his cell and had wallowed in the mud of the streets for a week. The mob halted below an illuminated oriel projecting from the dark palace wall, and with a shrill voice and the gestures of a town crier the woman yelled, "Harken and take notice, ladies and gentlemen! In a little while, the monk Astorre will slumber next to his wife Antiope." Boisterous laughter accompanied this proclamation.

Now the tinkling belled cap of Gocciola peeked forth from the narrow bay window of the oriel, and a melancholy face showed itself to the street.

"Good woman, be quiet," complained the fool tearfully to the plaza below. "You insult my upbringing and offend my sense of shame."
"Good fool," answered the shameless woman, "don't be irked by this! What the noble ones commit, we are calling by its name. We are putting the label on the druggist's bottle."

"By my deadly sins," exulted Serapion, "that we do! Until midnight the wedding of my little brother is to be rung out and proclaimed in all the plazas of Padua. Forward, march. Hut ho!" and he lifted his bare leg with its sandal out of the drooping tatters of the filthy habit.

This farce of the crowd subsided in the night against the steep walls of the palace, the windows and rooms of which for the most part faced the inner courtyard.

In a quiet, secluded chamber Antiope was being dressed and adorned by her ladies in waiting, Sotte and another, while Astorre received the seemingly never-ending stream of guests at the head of the stairs. She looked at her own anxious eyes, which faced her in a silvered mirror which was being held in bare, insolent arms by a maid with an envious face.

"Sotte," she said in a low voice to the servant who was braiding her hair, "you look like me and have my build: change clothes with me if you love me! Go and take the ring from her finger! Contrite and humbly! Bow down before the Pizzaguerra woman with crossed arms, like the least slave! Fall on your knees! Roll around on the floor! Abandon yourself utterly! Only get the ring from her! I will pay you a princely reward!" and as she saw Sotte hesitating: "Take and keep everything valuable which I am wearing!" pleaded the mistress, and the vain Sotte could not resist this temptation.

Astorre, who stole a moment from his duties as host in order to visit his love, found in the chamber two women exchanging clothes. He guessed.

"No, Antiope!" he forbade. "You cannot slide by like that. A word once given must be kept. I demand it of your love. I command it of you!" As he was turning this stern saying into an endearment by bestowing a kiss on the beloved neck, he was grabbed by Ascanio who had hurried thither to advise him that his peasants wanted to present their gifts to him without delay in order to begin their trip home in the cool of the night.   As Antiope turned to kiss her husband in return, she kissed the air.

Now she quickly finished dressing.   Even the frivolous Sotte was frightened by the pallor of the countenance in the mirror. Nothing was alive in it but the fear in the eyes and the sheen of the clenched teeth. A red streak, Diana's punch, became visible on the white forehead.

After the completion of her toilette, the wife of Astorre got up with a throbbing pulse and pounding temples, left her safe chamber and hurried through the rooms, looking for Diana. She was driven on by a spirit of dread. She wanted to hurry joyously back to her husband with the recovered ring, having spared him the sight of her humiliation.

Soon she distinguished from the crowd the mask of the tall goddess of the hunt, recognized in her her enemy, and followed, trembling and muttering angry words, her measured steps as she left the main hall and mercifully disappeared into one of the poorly lit adjoining rooms with low ceilings. The goddess apparently did not seek public humiliation, but rather a humility of the heart.

Now Antiope bowed before Diana in the half light. "Give me the ring!" she spat out and fumbled at the strong finger.

"Contrite and humbly?" asked Diana.

"How else, Lady?" said the unhappy one feverishly. "But you are playing with me, monster! You are bending your finger, now you've crooked it!"

"Was Antiope imagining things? Did Diana really make such sport? How slight is a crooked finger!

Cangrande, you have accused me of injustice. I shall not judge."

Enough, the Vicedomini raised her lithe body and cried, her flaming eyes fastened on the stern eyes of the Pizzaguerra, "Will you tease a married woman, maid?" Then she bent down again and tried with both hands to take the ring from the finger – and she was struck by lightening. Leaving the left hand to her, the avenging Diana drew with her right hand an arrow from her quiver and killed Antiope. The latter fell first on her left hand, then onto her right, twisted and lay down on her side, with the arrow in her neck.

The monk, who after the departure of his country guests came hurrying back and looked eagerly for his wife, found her lifeless. With a choked cry he threw himself down next to her and drew the arrow from her neck. A stream of blood followed. Astorre lost consciousness.

When he recovered from his faint, Germano was standing before him with his arms crossed. "Are you the murderer," asked the monk.

"I do not murder women," answered the other sadly, "It is my sister who sought her justice."

Astorre groped after the arrow and found it. Leaping up in a single movement and wielding the long shaft with its bloody tip like a blade, he attacked in a blind rage the playmate of his youth. The warrior shuddered slightly before the livid spirit dressed in black, with disheveled hair and the arrow in its fist.

He stepped to the side. Drawing his short sword, which he wore today, though unarmored, he blocked the arrow, and said compassionately, "Go back to your monastery, Astorre, which you should never have left!"

Suddenly he became aware of the tyrant, who came in through the door precisely opposite him, followed by all the celebrants, who had thronged to the gate to meet the long-awaited host.

Ezzelino stretched forth his right hand, bidding peace, and Germano lowered his weapon respectfully before his commanding officer. The wild monk seized the moment and stabbed Germano, who was focused on the tyrant, in the chest with the arrow. But himself he also hit fatally, as the lightening-fast sword of the warrior struck him.

Germano fell down without a sound. The monk, supported by Ascanio, made few more faltering steps towards his wife and, lowered by his friend, lay himself down next to her, mouth to mouth.

The wedding guests encircled the wedded pair. Ezzelino stood, contemplating Death. Then he got down on one knee and closed first Antiope's eyes, then Astorre's. In the stillness a raucous noise came in through the open window. One heard from the darkness, "Now the monk Astorre slumbers next to his wife Antiope." And distant laughter.

Dante arose. "I have paid for my place by the fire," he said, "and now seek the felicity of slumber. The Lord of Peace protect us all!" He turned and strode through the portal, which the page had opened for him. All eyes followed him, as he slowly climbed the steps of a torchlit stairway.

About the author

Conrad Ferdinand Meyer was born 1825 in Zurich. He is one of the most important German-language Swiss authors of the nineteenth century. A late-bloomer, his first literary success came when he was 46, with the publication of <u>Hutten's Last Days</u>. He was 50 when he married Luise Ziegler in 1875. He wrote many historical novellas, continuing to write until 1891. The University of Zurich awarded him an honorary doctorate degree in 1880. He died in 1898. The City of Zurich awards a prize in honor of Meyer to young Swiss artists (The Conrad-Ferdinand-Meyer-Preis).

About the translator

David Staats holds a Bachelor of Arts degree from Wesleyan University and a Juris Doctor from Harvard University. He lived in Germany for two and a half years, and has continued to study the language. He also is the translator of "Wave Propagation in Ionized Gases under the Influence of a Magnetic Field," by Wilhelm Altar, reprinted in *Proceedings of the American Philosophical Society*, vol. 126, no. 5, pp. 425-440 (1982).

Made in the USA
Middletown, DE
22 July 2018